# Over

# and

# Over Again

*Debut Novel from the Pen of*

*Ni'cola*

NCM Publishing
PUBLISHING

*NCM Publishing*

ISBN 978-0-578-01114-1
First Printing May 2009

*This is a work of fiction. It is not meant to depict, portray or represent any particular real persons. All the characters, incidents, and dialogues are the products of the author's imagination and are not to be construed as real. Any references or similarities to actual events, entities, real people, living or dead, or to real locales are intended to give the novel a sense of reality. Any similarity in other names, characters, entities, places, and incidents is entirely coincidental.*

Cover Layout & Design – Custom Eyes Studio
Editor – Shonell Bacon, Leila Jefferson

NCM Publishing
Las Vegas, NV 89108
www.ncmpublishing.com

# Dedication

This novel is dedicated to the ones that I hold so
very close to my heart, my children:

Destani Imani

Diamond Lynn

You are the wind beneath my wings... I truly love
you both. You're my inspiration...

And in loving memory of

Dionni Jewel

Sunrise January 6, 2003 – Sunset February 16,
2003

Thanks for making sure that mommy and your
sisters are okay..... I miss you.

# Acknowledgments

*First I would like to give honor to God*, through whom all things are possible. I would like to thank you for giving me the ability to complete this manuscript, and if He says the same, will allow me to complete many more.

*Destani and Diamond* you have been my inspiration in everything that I do. When I look into your eyes I get the strength to complete everything I have started. I want you to know that any thing is possible. You are my motivation everyday. You allow me to just out there, grind, and stay determined to make Over and Over Again a best seller.

*Mommy and Daddy* thanks so much for all of your support. Mommy you are the President of my street team…LOL… Mommy you have helped me out so much with promotion and pre-sales on the job, but most of all just spreading the word. Daddy thank you for just believing in me. That means more to me than all of the financial contributions that you have administered to me throughout my life…LOL.

*To all my sisters and brothers, but especially Janet, Sheila, Debbie, and NeNe* thank you for being such great motivators and telling me I can when everyone else says that I can't. Thank you for pushing me all through life in everything that I do. Thank you for all of those telephone conference calls providing sound advice and listening to all of my complaints.

Thank you the most for looking out for the girls

and me, even when you don't hear from me in a while. It takes a village to raise a child, and I can say that you guys have been my backbone through everything.

**_Big Mama and Big Daddy_** you are the best grandparents that I could ever have. Just knowing that someone loves you unconditionally and has so for all your life is a really good feeling. Thank you.

**_The Black Pearl of Fashions Ms C. LeFear_**, to whom I was privileged to have earned that C in my middle name from. What's your motto…? What can I say, If you got, you got it… I think I inherited my confidence and style from you. Ha Ha Ha… I love you. You are the best God/Grand Mother that anyone could ever have.

**_Andrice and Shardai_** thank you for just loving me. Dricie thank you for all of those text messages and calls you send just to say I Love You. They really mean so much to me. Dai, or should I say Lil' Nicki? You have always looked up to me, and when you were little, I am not gonna lie. You used to get on my nerves! Naw girl..LOL. It was just so cute how you mimicked everything that I did from school, dancing, no matter what I did, you did it too. Just like the girls, you are my motivation to strive to be a better person in life, and I love you forever.

**_Holly, Nyeisha, Taysia and Trish_** ya'll have been my girls and favorite cousins since day one. Thank you so much for loving me. Holly and Nyeisha we grew up like sisters and when you both moved away, that hurt my heart, but I am glad that our closeness never left.

Trish and Taysia as much trash that I may speak to you, its just a cover up of how proud that I am of both of you. You are my ice cream to my cake, my peanut butter to my jelly....LOL I love you. I really appreciate it all of your new zip codes because your houses are now my Motel 6's when I am in the area.

*Tina and Lisa* you have had my back through everything, and I know that both of you are tired of all my calls with tears, excitement, and complaints. Tina I love you for just believing in me and that is all that matters. When something is falling short, you jumps right in and handle it. You got me booked in so many places that between you and Tamika I need to invest in a buddy pass. Lol Everyone needs a Tina in their life.

Lisa, you are the only grown woman that I will let call me Boo-Boos. LOL. I love your genuine concern and take charge attitude when it comes to me and the girls. In the words of Tupac, you are appreciated.

*Cookie Monster* I have been calling you Cookie for so long that if anyone hears me refer to you as Dwayne they are like who? You are my nephew and the little brother that I never had... tear... Thank you for listening to me and working so hard for me running errands when I have an event or just at home. You are my personal assistant, and you work harder than any paid employee..

*Mama Cookie* wow, what can I say? You are one of the most phenomenal and inspirational women that I have ever met in life. You have been another mother to me for real.. When I am down, you always seem to come out of the woodwork, calling to say that I'm just checking on you. You okay? That is priceless. I love you so much.

**Wendy and Brenda** you two are the best adopted moms. I guess that's why I can't get out of line because I have all of these women making sure I succeed. Thank you for taking my children in and being better to them than some biological grandparents are in the world. I love you.

**My Annie's Pat and Doretha** ever since I was little, you always said that I was going to be somebody. Well I am trying to be the best somebody that you could have ever predicted…

**Ti Ti Zelma** man you have the best words of encouragement. Girl, you should work for Hall Mark! Anyway, I love all of our conversations and your tell it like it is attitude. I love you.

**Ms Fannie Mae** I would be tripping if I accidentally left you out. I love how you have stayed on me to live up to my potential. You have always stressed how much talent there is in this family, so I had to show the world mine. Thank you for being the superb aunt that you are. I love you.

**To all my aunts, uncles, cousins, nieces, and nephews** ya'll know that there are a gang of ya'll. There is so much genuine love in my family that it would take for ever acknowledging all of you. Just remember, without you I wouldn't be here.

**Dwayne Robinson** man you leave me speechless. You have had my back throughout this entire process. When I have an idea I always go to you first. You always formulate a plan to allow me to see that my thoughts and ideas can be a reality. You are the Vice President to the street team. You have assisted me in every way to make it happen. I love you and thank you.

*Steeve Washington* the baddest stylist in the land! You have been my big brother ever since we met damn near let me see ugh, over 20 years ago. You always make sure that I am okay. I believe that you are supposed to be in my life for a life time. Thank you for putting Over and Over Again on the map when it was still a thought in my head. Dude I love you.

*Ms. Earline and Mr. Eddy* thank you for loving the girls and I unconditionally. Thank you for believing in me and being proud of me. Ms. Earline thank you for all of those long talks we share. Mr. Eddy you were the first one who placed an order for the book. Little things like that means a lot.

*Ms. Downtown Brown*, thank you for sticking by my side and motivating me to write this book. You are my sister regardless of what changes life may bring. I love you.

*Jermial Smith* thank you for pushing me to get the story in my head out there. You are truly my motivator. You always push me to stay focus and complete every task that I take on. We might have our differences, but you have never turned your back on me. I love you Smith. Thank you.

*Ms. Sharonna Shelton* girl you are so beautiful. Thank you for making my cover come to life. When I first envisioned Dionni, you were the face that came to my head. I knew that you could make it come alive, but Damn! You blew everyone's hair back with those photos. Thank you for having my back and believing in me.

*Emika Porter* thank you for coming on short notice to create the look that I envisioned for Dionni. You were HUGE pregnant, and still came out to the shoot and styled Sharonna for me. You did your thing girl.

*Pamela Harper*, girl I can't STAND you!!! You know I'm kidding. You are the greatest proof reader, co-worker, friend, and confidant that anyone could have asked for. Your dry humor and constant sarcasm gets me through my day. You allowed me to believe that I can cuss out a grown person....LOL. Just joking...I love you Ms. Pamela.

*Irene, Cody, Kerry, and Kristy otherwise known as CRC*. Thank you first of all for welcoming and accepting me like family. I enjoy all of our laughs. Thank you educating me on how to become a successful business woman. You make coming to work so enjoyable. Without your warm words of encouragement, I don't believe that I would have even become serious about publishing this book. Thank you CRC.

*Kolanda Scott* as a PR consultant and my friend you have given me so much insight and knowledge on what I need to do to brand myself and my book. You are so direct and to the point, but at the same time has been a genuine friend. I thank you KO.

*KayBee of Custom Eyes Studio* you are a BEAST when it comes to the design game. You are a perfectionist and maybe the smartest man that I have ever met. You challenge my ideas, and together we have blown the minds of everyone who has come across my cover, designs, etc.

*Tamika Newhouse* of African American on the

Move Book Club it is always a pleasure. You have been a great friend and I appreciate all of the guidance that you have given me with the in's and out's of the book game.

*Peron F. Long* boy I know you are so tired of me will all those calls starting off "I have a question". You have been a great mentor, and I have given you the title of my "literary brother".

*Michael Lewis* when I first met you, I didn't know what to think. I still can't believe you wrote Memoirs of a Street Dream. But there goes to show, you can't judge a book by its cover. I still want to be the promoter of the Boys In the Hood Book Tour. I love you Papa. I am happy you adopted me as your God Daughter. You are one of my biggest supporters, and in turn I am yours.

*Theresa Gonsalves* thank you for welcoming me with so much love. Thank you for listening to me and giving me all of that wonderful information. Sometimes you need a friend doing the same thing that you are to understand you true feelings.

*Tina Brooks McKinney and Michelle Moorer* between the two of you I appreciate how you have extended your network to me. I listen to all advice and tips, I really do. Thank you for having so much faith in me and trusting that I can really do this.

*Loretta Walls* you know that I would be tripping if I did not say your name. You have been my role model every step of the way. God blessed me when he brought you into my life. Thank you.

*Marie Antoinette, Jessica Robinson, Sheila Lipsey*, and the host of other authors who have promoted me while promoting themselves, and ladies best believe I am doing the same. Thank you so much. We got to have each other's back and keep providing words of encouragement when the game gets frustrating.

*Who Does Your Hair Beauty Salon*, Toya thank you and your stylist for welcoming me in, and assisting in the process of promoting this book. You ladies are beautiful and are appreciated.

*Head Hunterz Barber Shop*, DT you have taken care of me and my girls from the beginning always going the extra mile. It touches my heart to know that there are still good black men out there. Thank you and your shop for promoting my novel.

*Modern Nails* you keep my eyebrows fly and my pedicures on point. Thank you promoting my book.

*All three phases of Master Piece Barber Shops, Upper Cuts, Hair Unlimited, Upper Cuts, Patricia's Hair and Nail Emporium, Iced Out Barber Shop*....Thank you for displaying my promo items in your shops.

*NPI Mountain Vista, NPI Rainbow, Summit Medical Group, and Healthcare Partners employees*.... Thank you for all the support and encouragement. Annette, Candice, and Reyna thank you for constantly calling me wanting updates of the status of this book. You all have displayed genuine concern and belief in this project. Thank you.

*Thank you to all my clients and friends*. There are so many of you out there, that I know I have not mentioned everybody, but I promise I will get you next round. Without all of you, I would not be anything, and I love you.

***And a final thank you to everyone*** who has preordered their copy of this novel. Thank you to everyone whom has joined the fan club and has taken the time to get to know me. My main goal was to get my story out there. I promise you, you will not be disappointed, and best of all. There is more to come.

# Chapter 1

"He has someone in here," Dionni said under her breath while she knocked on the door again. The knocking slowly intensified to banging while Dionni's girlfriends waited in her BMW that blocked the white, late-model Malibu parked in front of Dale's Lexus. All she had to do was give the signal, and her girls were ready for action.

Dionni walked to the front of the house and banged on Dale's window.

*This nigga is truly fucking with me*, she thought.

"Who is it?" she heard Dale yell from inside.

"It's me," Dionni answered, clenching her fist until the tips of her fingers turned white.

It didn't matter that it was 42 degrees outside; Dionni's growing anger kept her body temperature up. She walked back to the door and proceeded to bang again.

Dale's brother came to the door rubbing his eyes. "Dionni," he said, yawning, "it's 2:30 in the morning."

"Antwan, I know what time it is. I was here later

than this last night, so why is there a problem tonight?"

"Dale, come to the door," Antwan yelled while blocking Dionni's entrance into the house. Dale came to the door and nodded to Antwan. Antwan, still with a careful eye on Dionni, backed out of the way, but instead of going right to his room, he went left in the direction of Dale's room and the garage.

"Hey, baby," Dale said, trying to kiss her face. He eyed her sweater knit black and white striped Chanel tank dress and asked, "Where's your coat, baby? Aren't you cold?"

"No, nigga, I'm not cold, I'm mad," she barked at him, folding her arms on her chest. *Damn, do I look like a clown*, Dionni thought as Dale gently pulled her into the house closing the door behind her. *He got me oh so fucked up playing like he was asleep and didn't hear me banging like a lunatic.*

"Baby, you tripping for real," Dale said, sighing. "Don't you want to lie down and have me take that dress off you?"

Dale's mocha brown skin was so tight and inviting as he wrapped his arms around her and rubbed circles on her back. The hair on the back of Dionni's neck stood still, making her uncomfortable.

"Dale," she asked quietly, looking up into his deep brown eyes as he gently kissed her forehead, "why did Antwan go into your room?"

Dale's body suddenly tensed as that hated three letter word, "Huh?" came out of his throat. By the sudden nervousness in his voice, Dionni's feelings were confirmed. Dionni's 5'9, 158-pound frame was no match to Dale's 210-pound, 6'4, solid but muscular build, but she was ready to whoop this nigga's ass if he still had some bitch in here.

Fifty thousand things ran through her head as she tried to break free of the now vice grip lock he had on her.

"Move, shit," she yelled, wrestling with Dale. "Nigga, you think you slick, just be a man and keep that shit 100. If you got some bitch in here, just say that shit." Still fighting, Dionni accidentally dug her three-inch stiletto heel into Dale's right pinky toe.

"Fuck," he screamed, hopping on his left foot. "Your ass is tripping for real."

Dionni pushed past him and raced down the hallway leading to Dale's room and noticed Antwan rushing out the garage.

"What the hell are y'all doing?" Antwan said,

squinting as he searched for his brother. "Dionni, why is your ass in here disrespecting our house like this?" Antwan reached out to grab Dionni, but he wasn't quick enough as she ducked and grabbed the garage door.

She yanked it open and couldn't believe that her psychic abilities were correct. In the far left corner of the cold ass garage, huddled with only a sheet wrapped around her, was some dark skinned chick attempting to hide behind the weight bench.

"Be a woman, ma, and don't have a nigga make you hide. It is cold as hell up in here. I am not going to do anything to you. How am I going to be mad at a bitch, but not the nigga? Couldn't no nigga or no female have me hiding asshole naked."

Shivering, the embarrassed girl came out of her makeshift hiding place clutching the sheet and approached Dionni with her head held down. Her Diana Ross weave was covering her face, so Dionni couldn't see her eyes.

"I feel dumb as hell," she said under her breath, inching toward Dionni.

"Well, why the fuck is you hiding then if you feel stupid?" Dionni exclaimed, shaking her head, feeling no pity for this bitch.

By this time, Antwan and Dale were both standing in the doorway of the garage.

"I am sorry, Ashley," Dale said in a low voice, "but I told you I love my girl."

Dionni turned around, glaring at Dale. "Nigga, you call this love? You leaving your girl outside in the cold, and being all up in here trying to hide some broad you just got finished fucking? Wow, dude, that's love? Damn, I hate to see what you would do if you hated me."

Dionni turned back to the ebony, disheveled being trying to be quiet as she attempted to creep by.

"Naw, honey, hold on, hold on," Dionni said to her, holding out her arm and blocking the chick's way. "Ashley? That's your name? Are you the same Ashley that I spoke to on the phone two weeks ago BECAUSE you gave Dale a card bad mouthing me?" She cut her eyes at Dale. "Wow, I thought you said that there wasn't anything going on between you and him. And you, Bitch Made Ass Nigga, I thought you said that she was just some ghetto rat at work that was stalking you? How long has this been going on?" Dionni asked Dale, but then quickly shook her head. "I don't care to know, I'm cool."

Dionni pushed the garage door button to open

the door and dashed out, bending down so the door didn't hit her in the head. Once outside, she turned and shook her head again. "Ashley, you can have him. You want him so badly, have him. I ain't going to go to jail for no bitch or no dick, but I promise you this, next time you have anything to say about me, best believe there will not be any fighting going down. I got a good fire arms card and will shoot your broke ass, do you feel me?"

Giving her attention to Dale, she said, "Baby, over the past six years of our relationship, you can't seem to keep your dick to yourself. You keep on fucking up over and over again, but damn, Daddy, for real, if you are going to cheat, why can't the bitch be on the same level as me or greater? Why do all of your pigeons have to be low budget? But, I guess you are upgrading because at least this one has a vehicle, even if it is busted."

Dionni whipped around, quickly dashing past Dale's truck and hopping into her car, trying to make sure that Dale did not see her cry. She placed her head onto the steering wheel and started to bawl. *This shit is not really happening.*

Dionni was so confused and hurt that she could

not breathe. All kinds of things were running through her head. She couldn't believe that only four hours ago she couldn't wait to see this man and finish what was started the night before.

While she was back at home admiring herself in her full length mirror, she was confident that all eyes would be on her as she walked up the steps to Poetry Nite Club on the Las Vegas Strip. The dress cupped her full but firm rump, ending an inch under it while the low cut of the front obsequiously showed her 36 D breast.

Her red leather 3/4 quarter-calf Manolo boots and fire red Dior leather satchel complemented the outfit. As she smiled, she applied her favorite perfume *Be Delicious* by Donna Karen. She slowly gave herself a final look over. Her honey brown hair was immaculate and full of body as it hung gently down to the middle of her back.

"David did his thang with that flat iron today," she said as she admired the straightness and fullness of her natural tresses. Her big hazel eyes shined with a thin dark brown line of Mac eye liner which lined her bottom lids. The black mascara on her lashes displayed the brightness of her eyes, and her caramel skin glistened as if she was still wet with the right amount of baby oil applied.

She kissed the mirror with her full lips and a sheer lining of her lip gloss was left there as she said, "Dale is going to have fun with my tipsy ass tonight when I leave the club and join him in bed." She giggled to herself and went downstairs to meet her friends.

"I hope he's okay and nothing happened to him," Dionni said under her breath as Tiana glanced up the stairs in disgust. She has been texting Dale all day and it was so unusual for him not to respond. Negative thoughts started to go through her head, but she shook them off. *If I do not hear from him by the time I leave the club, then I'll start to trip,* she thought to herself.

"Damn, girl," Tiana said, "we thought you had second thoughts about the club again and was going to go and cupcake with that Dale." She gently placed Dionni's puppy Dior on the ground and pulled on her jeans. "You know I can't have dog fur on these apple bottoms." She said while looking at her booty in the mirror.

"Well, you know it always takes me awhile to get dressed, and no I ain't change my mind, heifer. My baby knows I'm coming over after the club." She gave Dior a Puppy Popcorn.

Tingling from excitement, sensations went through Dionni's body from the thoughts of being with Dale the night before. Her body still shook from anticipation from just that morning when he called her and said, "Dionni, I need you right now."

She jumped up and hopped in the shower. She quickly bathed in his favorite fragrance from Vicky Secrets, Love Spell, and hurried up and patted herself dry. She mixed the matching lotion with some baby oil and caressed her entire body, imagining Dale's strong hands, and she felt warmth between her legs.

"Hold on, Sexy," she told her friend as she gently rubbed a pinch of baby oil on her clitoris. "We will be there in a minute." She unwrapped the silk scarf from her hair and brushed her hair down and around her shoulders. She brushed her teeth and washed her face. Once she was finished, and hurried past the bed she rushed to her closet, only to be interrupted by the ringing of her cell phone again.

"Damn, baby, have you left yet?" Dale's smooth and low baritone voice swooned on the other line.

"Yes, baby, I'm in the car right now," she lied crossing her fingers, hoping that her three-month-old

Pomeranian did not wake up and give her away by barking.

"Okay, baby, please come on. Daddy is waiting for Sexy to come place her fruits and berries on him, and by the way, I'm missing you, too."

"Okay, then tell Daddy I'm almost there, just unlock the door. I got a surprise for you."

Flinging her phone on the bed, Dionni got her long Coach trench coat out of the closet and wrapped it around her naked body. Stepping into some fuchsia stilettos she got from Wild Pair a couple of months ago, she chuckled recalling her statement that the shoes were going to be labeled her crack in case of an emergency hooker heels.

She got her keys, kissed Dior on the head, and placed her into her kennel. She then charged down the stairs and got into her eggshell white 745 BMW. She started it up and proceeded on her journey to join her baby while turning off her leather seat heaters. Even though it was late December and so cold that ice was hanging off branches, she was warm from anticipation and didn't need the heat her seats provided.

When she got close to Dale's subdivision, she turned down Dionne Farris' "Hopeless" and applied some fruity lip gloss to her lips. She parked her car behind his truck and walked up the driveway to his front door. She tried the door and it was locked, so she rang the doorbell.

After a brief moment, Antwan appeared at the door with a dingy wife beater on and some green boxer shorts. His baby dreads were sticking up all over the place, looking like spiders dancing on his head.

"Hey, Dionni, what's good wit' it?" he asked, scratching between his legs.

"Nothing much," she replied as she waited for him to let her in. *Oh, I can't stand that no home training ass nigga,* she thought. She marched through the door, and as she walked to Dale's room, she could feel Antwan's eyes on her booty.

When she entered his room, she smiled at the love of her life.

"Dale," she said quietly, gently tapping on his shoulder. He was sprawled out across the bed with the cell phone still in his hand. He wore a pair of blue checkerboard Sean John boxers which complemented his thick muscular thighs.

He nudged a little bit, but didn't awaken. She kneeled on the bed beside him and tried to turn him over onto his back. "Dale," she called again, just a little louder than before. This time he responded by groaning and opening his eyes a tad. "Damn, baby, you know I been trying to wait up for you. What took you so long?"

Dionni placed a well manicured finger up to Dale's mouth and whispered, "Shh, I got something for you that will make up for your waiting period." Dionni reached over Dale and grabbed the remote. She turned on the soul station on his satellite television.

The sweet voice of Adrian Hood swooned through the surround sound, singing "Brown Eyed Blues." This was one of Dionni's grooves, and she started to sway to the beat. Dale opened his eyes wide, pushing himself back and propping up onto the pillows. He wanted to see what exactly she had in store for him.

Dionni slowly unbuttoned her jacket while singing softly, "I just want to hold her hand, be her man, and hope that she takes the chance…" She had her eyes closed tightly as she continued to sing, sway, and unbutton the fourth button. Even though Dale and Dionni had been together for six years, his body still rose to attention by just admiring her beauty and femininity. Dale started to rub the growing bulge that appeared through his shorts as Dionni slowly approached him.

Dionni placed her hand tenderly on top of Dale's and gracefully took over what he was trying to start. She continued to unbutton her jacket until it was clear that she was completely naked underneath. She continued to keep a grip on his manhood periodically getting tighter as she sped up the pace. Taking off her jacket with her free hand, Dionni bent down and nibbled on the head of his dick.

Dale watched in anticipation, hoping that she would take his thick nine inches into her mouth. Dionni could tell what he wanted by the deep breaths he began to take and how his body was bouncing to her rhythmic beat. She sucked his dick like a champ, occasionally spitting on it, which seemed to be turning him on even more by the sound.

When she noticed his eyes rolling into the back of his head, Dionni quickly stood and pulled Dale into his adjourning bathroom. With her heels still on, Dionni bent over the sink, placing one hand onto the counter. She rubbed her clitoris with the other and purred out to Dale, "Please come and fuck me."

Grabbing her full hips, Dale kept the tip of his dick right at the opening of Dionni's pussy as he teased her, rubbing it up and down her lips, and around the mouth of her well shaven treasure chest.

"Baby, you still have those heels on," he said, glancing down to her feet, "you know that shit turns me on." Suddenly, he picked up Dionni from behind and placed her in a kneeling position onto the sink.

Dionni reached out for the vanity mirrors. "What the hell are you doing?" she asked, her voice high with excitement.

"It's your turn to be quiet," he said as he separated his second favorite mouth on her body and started to kiss and lick gently. He continued on until her pussy created its own foam of cum. Dionni's body gyrated on the sink. "Hold on, baby, don't fall," he said softly and held her ankles steady. He got onto the tips of his toes and shoved his dick into her.

Tears came to Dionni's eyes as she held on for dear life to the wall and the mirror. Dale continued to give her full long strokes, making her cum over and over again.

"Damn, Daddy, I love you so much," she exclaimed between grunts and moans. Dale held onto her hips tightly as he pushed one last time and finally came, burying his head into her back.

Kissing her left ass cheek first, then the right, Dale finally responded, "Baby, I love you, too."

By this time, they were so tired they barely made it back into Dale's bed. Dale held Dionni tightly for the rest of the night, and in the morning promised that they were going to continue round two after she came back in from a night on the town with her girls.

Sitting up, Dionni tried to shake off all thoughts of what happened last night. She stared out the windshield, looking at nothing.

*I can't believe I let him do this to me again,* she thought, fighting hard to keep her tears in check.

Dale's last act of infidelity occurred seven months ago, and Dale promised that he was never going to cheat on her again; Dionni had heard that story so many times before. She wanted to kick her own ass for taking him back yet again.

"Girl, do you want me to choke that bitch out real quick and use the bammer on that nigga?" Tiana asked Dionni while rubbing on her back. "He truly is not worth the tears, you know this, right? You are so much better than this situation right here."

Wiping the tears away with the back of her hand, Dionni looked at her friend and sighed. "You are right, girl. They ain't worth it. I am just so tired of going through this shit. I don't know what is wrong with me. I know I am too worthy to deal with the drama that I keep receiving from Dale, but just like Anthony Hamilton said, I can't let go."

Eva reached over from the back seat and tried to rub Dionni's hair back into place. "You know what it is that keeps you taking that chocolate man back. You ain't ADD, but ADDD, Addicted to Da Delicious Dick!" Wiping the tears away, Dionni started to chuckle and finally all three of them busted out laughing as Eva said, "That bitch was not in the garage though, looking like a ghetto Mufasa with that lion's mane she called hair. Girl, you know my motto, don't chase 'em, replace 'em. Give him something to worry about and don't call him. Let's go to Denny's for some breakfast."

"I love you guys, you know that, right?" Dionni said, glancing at both of her girls.

"Well, show us by paying for this good ole meal that we are about to receive," Tiana said, giggling and turning up the radio. "Serve us up like Raheem says." She bounced to the music.

Dionni shook her head, and as she pulled off, she thought, *If he calls, don't answer for a couple of days.*

She put her attention onto the road and continued her journey to Denny's to feed her girls.

# Chapter 2

"Damn, Dior," Dionni exclaimed as she noticed the chewed heel of her brown Jimmy Choo's. "Dior is going to have to get it together, or she is going to be homeless." Dionni had those particular shoes in mind when she picked the outfit for her meeting with a new client.

At 27, Dionni was a very successful event planner. With her company, Whateva You Like Entertainment, she conducted the majority of her business out of her home office, but she leased an entire office building that she transformed into different themed fantasy rooms. She hosted everything from kid's birthday parties to weddings.

After grabbing another pair of shoes out of her closet, Dionni jumped into her car and raced onto the expressway. She called Tiana at the office to give her a heads up that she was going to be late.

"Good morning, we are here to give you whatever you like. This is Tiana. How may I help you?"

"Hey, girl, it's me," Dionni said into her cell phone. "I just wanted to give you a heads up that I am running a little late. My heel broke on my Jimmy's."

"Well, your 10 am appointment is here and on time," Tiana replied professionally into the phone giving Dionni the impression that the client must be in her face. "Is there anything in particular you want me to do or tell him?" Tiana was impressed by how well this brother looked with his 6'2 athletic frame draped in a designer suit and gray gators.

"I told him," Tiana began, whispering, "that this is whatever you like, and I am feeling like TI with that song and want to give him whatever he likes."

"Girl, you are crazy, I am almost there." Dionni laughed as she hung up.

Tiana smiled and patted the waves on her new Keyshia Cole hair cut. She stood, fixed her skirt, and offered the fine brotha some brochures to look at and refreshments.

"Mr. Grey," she said, "Dionni is finishing up with another client and will be here momentarily. We have water and coffee in the back and a box of crispy creams if you would like. Just let me know if there is anything that I can do to be of service to you." She gave him an award-winning smile

*I haven't dated any men with hair since college, but damn, this Indian looking nigga is fine as hell*, she thought.

"No, ma'am, I am fine," the handsome gentleman told Tiana. "And please don't call me Mr. Grey. That was my father. My name is Zay," he said in a low voice making her panties moist.

"Ok, Mr. Zay," she purred back at him. "I will be right here if you need me." Tiana sauntered off into the back, shaking what her mama gave her.

Even though she was attracted to Zay, Tiana prayed that this man might just be Dionni's knight in shining armor. When David called her from the hair salon earlier that day and informed her of his plan, she hoped it would worked. Dionni was a good person and deserved to be happy.

Tiana's thoughts evaporated as she watched her girl rush into the office.

"Hello, Mr. Grey," Dionni said in a professional but sexy tone, glancing up and down at the man ahead of her.

*Wow, it's going to be hard working with him,* she thought. Smiling, she extended her right hand. "My name is Dionni Stone, and I am the owner of Whateva You Like."

Something about the man excited Dionni. He

had the appearance of an intelligent business man, but his attitude displayed the slight cockiness of a thug. It was hard for Dionni to hold back because that was the type of man that she liked.

"Yes, Dionni, it is nice meeting you," Zay replied, shaking her hand with his right, but running his left over his hair. His wavy reddish brown hair was pulled back in a tight ponytail that fell to the middle of his back.

"Like I told your assistant, my father was Mr. Xavier Grey, and I would like to be called Zay."

"Well alrighty then," she said through a smile, showing off her perfectly white teeth. "Zay," she said, now nervous of the fact that he was still holding onto her hand.

Turning around and trying to lift the awkwardness that appeared in the air, Dionni said, "So you want to plan a graduation party for your sister? Do you know what theme you want? I suggest a white linen event, but just like the name, you can have whatever you like."

Dionni walked over to the table, glancing back making sure that Mr. Fine had his eyes on the sway of her size 9 thick hips.

Dionni purchased her brown and teal suit from Anne Taylor just for this meeting. She had been excited and nervous in anticipation of this day and hoped that Zay liked *the presentation* she was displaying. She knew that everything had to be perfect since she found out about Zay from her hairdresser David.

David was the owner of Screaming Heads Hair and Day Spa. He had been Dionni's beautician since she moved to Vegas back in college. When David explained that his investment banker was trying to plan a surprise graduation party for his little sister, Dionni jumped on the chance to take on the project. When David went on to explain to Dionni how important the party was to Zay because he raised his sister by himself after their parents died in a house fire, not only did she want to take on the project, but she wanted to make it as beautiful as she could.

"Girl, if the nigga was gay, I would be his fun boy," David confessed. "He is fine as fuck. His people is from Louisiana and he Creole mixed with French and shit. "G-u-r-l!" David had to stop straw setting her hair so that he could fan himself.

"Just hook a nigga up. I told him that I know a bitch that can handle his shit, and, girl, I know that you can do it in more ways than one! I am tired of seeing you go back to that loser, Dale. He doesn't know what he got in you, so I think that Xavier Grey can get your mind off of the Mandingo."

David and Dionni high-fived each other and laughed. Once they calmed down, he went back to hooking her head up.

Watching him watch her, Dionni could see why David was so excited bout dude. *He definitely is sexy,* she thought. *But let me see where his head is at, and then take it from there.*

Dionni was a true believer in faith, and she believed that everyone who stepped into her life had been placed there for a reason. It has been five months since the last time that she has seen Dale, and she truly believed that it was about time for her to start showing interest in the opposite sex.

"Here are some examples of some white linen events that I have coordinated, not just in Vegas, but across the country," she said. "We can have the event here, or if you would like, at any of the major hotels on the strip. I have ongoing contracts with most of the major ones, so it would be at a reasonable rate. Follow me into my office, and we can discuss numbers."

Glancing down at the diamond encrusted Cartier watch he wore on his left hand, Zay explained to her that he had another engagement already scheduled. He really wanted to hear the rest of her ideas though and wanted to know if they could continue the meeting at dinner later that night.

"Do you like Mediterranean food? I'll have my assistant make a reservation at Olives in the Bellagio. It has a casual dress code. Bring some of your books along. We can discuss numbers there among some other things. How does that sound?"

Dionni tilted her head to the left and smiled. "I would love to join you. I will see you there."

Dionni didn't understand why this man was sending a sensation to "Sexy" the way that he was, but she had to remind herself and *Mz. Sexy* that this was just business. If it turned out to be pleasure later on, then she was not going to stop it, but for right now, she had to put on her game face and get all of her best samples together for the dinner.

"It was nice meeting you, sir," Dionni told him. She stood and escorted him to the door. She watched him walk to his 2008 Jaguar S-Type and get in.

Tiana walked up behind her and said, "Boss

Lady, that nigga right there--- if you don't want him, I'll take him. Shit, I just want to see how sturdy those rubber bands are keeping all that hair in place while I'm holding on enjoying that ride." Tiana grinned her ass off.

"Girl, you crazy," Dionni said, laughing. "That's why I love yo ass. You got to excuse me, mamacita. I got to make sure this presentation is on point."

Dionni went off into her office, rattling off a list of tasks that she was going to need completed for her meeting tonight.

"Welcome to the Bellagio," the valet attendant told Dionni as she stepped out of her car in a pair of tan slacks and a beige tunic top. Her French manicure was fresh and shining through her gold stiletto sandals that matched her gold Fendi purse. She sported a gold Coach briefcase and her hair was pulled back into a clip.

"Be careful with my baby," she said through a smile and walked gracefully to the entrance of the hotel.

As she found her way to the restaurant, she knew that she was turning heads. Her attire was sophisticated but sexy, and she hoped that Zay liked it.

At the main entrance of Olives, Zay was waiting, looking pretty fine himself. He was wearing the shit out of a green and white Iceberg warm up suit with a pair of green and white fusions on his feet. His hair and goatee sported a fresh line, and he wore a gold Movado watch on his wrist.

Dionni was impressed and reached in to the friendly embrace that was waiting for her. "Damn, you smell good," Zay told Dionni while taking in another whiff.

"Thank you, sir," she replied, turning her head to hide the sudden color that appeared in her cheeks. "So do you. Is that Versace Blue Jeans you have on?"

Zay nodded, impressed by her observation and signaled for the hostess.

"Grey, party of two," he said to the attendant while admiring Dionni. *I hope I can keep my composure during this meeting,* he thought. *I thought David was just hyping her up, but this chick is definitely wifey material.*

The hostess signaled for them to follow.

Over dinner, Dionni impressed Zay once again by her samples of linen and pictures of events that she hosted from famous artists in the music industry to ball players.

Dionni was definitely on point, and Zay was falling for her more and more as she spoke. He could not take his eyes off of her and wondered why she was single.

When David described how wonderful Dionni was as an events planner, he made sure to mention that she was beautiful and single.

*Whoever the brother was that let this catch go, man, I am so sorry, but it is totally his loss.* So many things were going through his head as he took in her every word and feminine gesture.

She articulated her words which showed that she was an educated woman, yet, her entire vibe stated that she was not to be fucked with.

Dionni was excited, but at the same time nervous of the feelings that she was having. Yes, she had promised herself that she was going to leave Dale alone and move on, but

at that moment, she kind of felt like she was cheating on him.

*Girl, let him go,* she told herself admiring the man in front of her. *You concentrate on you, and just go with the flow. Have fun, and ride this shit till the wheels fall off.*

At the end of dinner, Zay assured her that he definitely wanted to render business with her and handed her a $5000 check for a deposit.

"You can email me all of the contracts, and I will forward them to my lawyer. If he agrees, then it will be lovely doing business with you," Zay said. "So do you really think that you can have all of what you explained done in a week and a half? I am leaving later on this week to the ATL for her graduation. She has a trip planned, so everything has to be done in an expedited manner."

Dionni stood, smiled, and said, "Just like the name says, you can have whatever you like, and that is how I conduct my business. I will guarantee that everything is what you like. I give you my word, it will be done."

# Chapter 3

"Nigga, pass that blunt this way," Dale told Twan. He was trying to concentrate on whooping Jermaine's ass while playing Madden 09, but fucked up and lost his turn.

The four of them were in the game room of Dale and Twan's house smoking, drinking, eating, and shooting the shit while having a miniature Madden tournament.

"Nigga, have you spoken to D?" Twan asked his brother while handing him the blunt.

"Yeah, she started answering the phone for me a couple of weeks ago, but she still not talking to me."

A week after Dionni left him cold and in the garage with his hood rat chick, he arrived at Dionni's house with a present for her and Dior.

When he got there, Dionni was on the couch asleep and Eva let him in. He walked up to her and gazed down at his sleeping beauty. Her hair was pulled back into a messy ponytail, and she wore no makeup. She was cradling the puppy who was also fast asleep in her arms.

They both looked so beautiful and peaceful,

which made Dale really start to feel like shit. He could not believe how he constantly puts his relationship with his Queen on the line.

He bent down and kissed Dionni on the forehead. Her eyes fluttered, and she smiled briefly seeing that it was Dale. After coming back to reality, Dionni jumped up and demanded to know why the hell he was standing in her living room.

"Where's Eva?" she asked him, gripping Dior and awaking the puppy. Startled, Dior started to bark at Dale. "You turned my puppy against me?" he said, not believing how angry and vicious Dior looked. "Well, I guess since you both hating on a brotha right now, you don't want these gifts I got for you."

Reaching down into the bag that he carried, he pulled out a platinum diamond encrusted Christian Dior necklace for her and a matching dog collar for Dior.

At first, Dionni's eyes widened and a smile came across her beautiful face while she jumped up to show it off to Eva, but the reminder of what happened came back to her.

Quickly, Dionni whipped around and stated, "Gifts like this is what usually have me bought whenever you mess up. I stopped complaining about it and just go with the flow, but this time, Dale, I am tired. Baby, really I am. I know I deserve better than this shit here. I know for a fact that if you cannot be the real man that I need you to be there are other men out there that would be happy to fulfill your role."

She walked off going up the stairs, leaving the jewelry pieces on the table.

Dionni had never acted like that when Dale tried to apologize. Her change of heart had his mind really going.

Defeated, Dale left quietly leaving the jewelry behind. At first he wanted it to be a peace offering, but after Dionni cut him in half with those powerful words, Dale realized Dionni deserved the jewelry for just putting up with his ass this long.

"She ain't never trip out this long, Twan, for real," he replied, shaking his head.

"I can't believe that shit happened five months ago."

Dale really believed that Dionni was done. In the past she would have given in by now. He'd apologize and they would be right back together. This time it was totally different.

Dale loved Dionni, but he also loved the smell

and feel of other women just as much.

He knew, without a doubt, that he had a bad bitch when it came to Dionni, and it was just not her looks.

She was a complete package from looks to brains, and she was also a monster in the bedroom. She had the presentation of a professional business woman, but at the same time had no problem demonstrating the Caribbean side of her and pulling her pink 9-millimeter on you if she thought you were fucking with her. She had no kids, which was so uncommon nowadays, and most important, she loved Dale unconditionally.

That's why he just did not know why when the opportunity struck he could not keep his dick to himself. For the first couple of months after the jewelry incident, he was calling her and sending lilacs to her office and home everyday. This had been the longest they had been apart, and he was missing her like crazy.

Some nights he felt like he was going crazy and said fuck it, "She *is* going to talk to me." Dale would then get up and make that fifteen-minute trek over there to her crib, just to get no response. He would ring her doorbell over and over again. Once again defeated, Dale would leave.

He went to her office, and every time he showed up there Tiana would tell him, "Sorry, sir, you just missed her," with a smirk on her face. The sly remark and gesture would only piss Dale off even more. He could not believe that Dionni had everyone involved to ensure her being MIA.

His last resort was to go to the dog park where Dionni usually took Dior. After two weeks of sitting on the bench, he spotted Eva getting out of her car with Dior in tow. He waited until they entered the small dog section and asked Eva, "Where is Dionni?" Sighing loudly and shaking her head, Eva informed him that Dionni was out of the country. She and her sisters flew to Jamaica for two weeks for a vacation and she was babysitting Dior.

Defeated again, Dale went home.

Even though Dale missed his woman and his "Sexy," Dale was still a man. He still fucked other bitches out of control. He convinced himself that when he and Dionni got back together he would give it up. But for now, he had to do him.

Four months after the garage episode, Dale showed up to Dionni's mother's house to plead with Ms. Asha to have her daughter call him. She lived in an exclusive neighborhood, owning a half-million dollar house that Dionni bought for her as incentive to move to Vegas.

Turning into her subdivision, Dale got nervous when he spotted Dionni's car leaving. Part of him wanted to follow her, but he felt that if he spoke to her mother first, then maybe she could tell him what approach that he should use to get her daughter back.

Dale spoke to Ms. Asha and told her everything that happened. He wanted to leave out some parts, but as close as he knew Ms. Asha was with all of her girls, he knew it would be better to come clean. Ms. Asha listened intensively to everything Dale had to say.

When he was finished, her words were short but to the point. "Well, it takes a real mon to speak from da heart," her Jamaican accent boomed. "But I don't know what you want fi'me to do for you? I will tell her to call you but, son, dats my daughter first, and I am always on her side. Get it together, bwoy," she told him, with her accent sounding as if she just got off the plane from Kingston.

She stood and hugged Dale. He loved Ms. Asha like she was his own mother even though the first time he met her he could not believe that Dionni was her child. Dionni was excited that her mother had finally decided to move to Vegas and chatted about her non stop till they reached the airport.

Once they arrived, he parked in short term parking and had to get change for the parking meter. Rushing to baggage claim, they found Dionni's mother flirting with a TSA agent. She wore hip hugging Citizen jeans and a baby white t-shirt with white clogs, looking more like an older sister than a mother.

The two women shared everything from the same skin tone to caring smile, and since that day Dale had catered to that woman just as much as he did her daughter. He knew that if anyone could talk to Dionni, it could be her.

Soon after leaving Ms. Asha's house, Dale was on the 115 freeway heading home. His cell phone rang, and "Me and My Girlfriend" by Tupac rang out in the car. Dale smiled, thanking the Lord when he looked down at his phone. Beside Dionni's name was a picture of her posing from the back in some purple boy shorts. He pushed the button on his blue tooth and said, "What's good with it?" as sexy as he could.

"That was a low blow trying to turn my momma against me," Dionni's voice came through Dale's earpiece soft but clearly. "What can I do for you?"

Every day, Dale had rehearsed exactly what he was going to say to Dionni if he ever got a chance to speak to her again, but now that the time had finally come he was dumbstruck.

"Ugh, I wanted to know if I could see you," he started off. "Baby, I know that I have messed up. I know that you are tired of my constant apologies and lies. You proved your point. I am lost without you. I have been walking around in a daze. I need you badly. D, I feel so incomplete without you."

Dionni listened to everything he had to say. Once he was finished, there was an awkward pause in between them. Dionni broke the silence by informing him that her phone was beeping and that she would call him back.

Dale was in shock when he heard the phone click in his ear and everything go silent. Since then, he had attempted to call her on so many occasions. She would always answer, and after exchanging hellos she would soon get an excuse to get off the phone.

Dale shook his head as his boys looked at him. They knew that Dionni was a dime, and all of them would have hit that shit a long time ago with as much fucking up Dale had done. But, she was a real woman and would never disrespect Dale like that.

"Well, a nigga ain't getting nothing but older, and I am ready to be a man for her," Dale told his boys. "If we get back right, I am going to ask her to marry me. I know that she got to believe that I am changing after I come to her with a fat ass rock."

The doorbell rang and Twan went to answer it. The men could hear the clicking of heels coming down the wood steps, and in came Alisha, one of Twan's girls and three of her home girls. All talks of Dionni subsided as the ladies got comfortable with the men around the room.

Nia was one of Alicia's girls and boldly sat her ass on Dale's lap. Dale momentarily forgot his love speech on Dionni as he whispered into Nia's ear, telling her how he needed to cum. She stood, pulling him up, and led him up the stairs to his room.

# Chapter 4

*I wondered what happened?* Tiana thought. She just entered the Blue Martini and was trying to find Dionni in the crowd.

Tiana was been at home, listening to jazz and painting her toenails. She knew Dionni was at her dinner meeting and was surprised when Dionni called, interrupting her pedicure session.

"T, can you meet me at our spot?" Dionni asked her in melancholy voice. "I need to talk to you."

"Okay, ma," Tiana replied finishing up on her left pinky toe. "Let me throw on something really quick. Give me 'bout 30 minutes. Where are you? Do you want me to stop and pick you up? Are you okay?"

Tiana wasn't sure what happened. *If this nigga did something out of line-.* Her thoughts were interrupted by Dionni telling her she was already on the strip.

"Ok, girl, see you in a few."

Forty-five minutes later, Tiana was looking for Dionni in the crowded bar. She found her in back of the patio, downing a Strawberry Martini.

Sitting there, Dionni appeared okay, but when she stood to greet her friend with a hug, Tiana could tell just the opposite. Her eyes and cheeks were red and swollen from crying. Hugging Dionni reminded Tiana of all the times the shoe was on the other foot. Dionni had always been the one to lean on, and Tiana was the one needing the shoulder.

Tiana soothed her friend and told her everything was going to be okay. Whatever it was. Pulling back from the embrace, Dionni started to chuckle in between her tears as she noticed tears forming in Tiana's eyes. "Girl, don't be crying because of my crazy butt. You don't even know what is wrong with me. Who would have thought that after everything we have been through, we would still be so close."

When Dionni hurt, so did Tiana, and vice versa. They have been friends for so long, that they could read each other's emotions without the other one having to say a word. Tiana almost broke this bond when she allowed Rashied, her ex fiancé, to keep them separated. He had such a hold on her that she was blinded to his cheating ways. She hung on to his every word and did everything that he wanted her to do. She was forever grateful that after she discovered his sex-a-pade with two of his students, Dionni welcomed her back with open arms.

Even though Tiana had been Dionni's assistant for the past three years, their friendship went all the back to college. The pair met on the campus of the University of Nevada, Las Vegas. Back then, they shared a dorm room and did not always get along very well. The waitress walked up, handing Tiana a menu. She asked the ladies if they were ready to order. Dionni nodded, and without looking at the menu, informed the waitress that they wanted two more Strawberry Martinis.

"This is still an open tab, so keep them coming please," Dionni said and then turned her attention back to Tiana.

"So, what happened?" Tiana asked as the waitress walked away. "You did not interrupt my boot leg spa treatment just to sit up and drink with me. Spill the beans, girl, before I got to go back to my roots and get ghetto with you."

Dionni chuckled as thoughts of the day that they met floated into her head. Dionni, originally from Jersey, was the youngest of four sisters. Her eldest sister Desi flew down with Dionni to help her get settled in. The two of them were unpacking and organizing her stuff when they heard a commotion in the hallway.

"Damn, where is 370 at?" a ghetto voice called

out. "This is crazy, don't no one know shit around here, but I know this, I better not be shacking with no white bitch!"

Tiana was from Omaha, Nebraska, and was hood rich. At the time, she believed that men weren't ballers unless they wore Shirley Temple curls or crimps in their hair.

"Girl, remember you had all those colors braided into your hair?" Dionni asked Tiana, laughing so hard she was crying. "You know I'm your girl, but who told you that shit was cute? Your whole outfit looked like something ShaNayNay would have worn."

That day, Tiana had a gold hoop ring in her nose and identical earrings. She had on a jean skirt with some knock off Manolo Timberland boots. Her bright orange tube top matched the tube socks she wore and the bangles on her arms. After giving her the once over, Dionni realized that this was going to be an interesting year.

Starting to laugh herself, Tiana remembered how Dionni and Desi stood there with their mouths wide open in shock at her entrance. Living in Jersey, she knew that they had to have seen project chicks with two-tone weaves and shit, but none of them broads could have prepared them for Tiana.

"I know I was a hot-mess back then," Tiana said, wiping the tears from her eyes. "I bet Desi was scared to leave, huh? But the first step is admitting, so here I go...." Standing up, Tiana held her right hand into the air. Looking Dionni dead in the eyes, she said in between laughs, "My name is Tiana, and I am ghetto as hell!"

People were turning around looking at them, wondering what was going on. Dionni laid her head down into her folded arms, cracking up laughing.

"Okay folks. The show is over," Tiana said waving her hands at her audience. "Now that I got you laughing, tell Mommy what is wrong with the baby." Tiana turned her attention back to Dionni and grew serious.

Trying to calm herself down, Dionni shook her head at Tiana, wondering if she was going to make sense when she attempted to explain to her friend what was on her mind.

"Well, let me start off by saying that you made me feel better just that quick," Dionni told Tiana, wiping the tears away. "But, girl, I am cool. I am just tripping thinking about Dale and Zay at the same time."

"What do you mean thinking about Dale and Zay?" Tiana asked, looking confused. "What happened? Why are you saying both of their names in the same sentence? I am so confused right now."

"He got this debonair presence about him. You know I landed the deal with Zay. He is so smart and funny. I was trying to concentrate on my salad, but I couldn't help but watch him eat his."

"So what is the problem?" Tiana interjected, really confused now. "You are always cool and collected, Dionni. Don't know how handle you this distraught."

"The problem is," Dionni began, staring at her drink, "I feel like I am cheating on Dale. I know I did not do anything wrong, but I would be lying to you if I said that I am not feeling really guilty right now. Zay was a complete gentleman the entire time, even though I didn't want him to be," she added with a smile. "But I feel like I am sneaking behind Dale's back. I know I need to get over this shit and let it go, but, girl, it is so hard. I don't know what to do right now."

Eva walked up to the table. Just like Tiana, Dionni and Eva had been friends for many years, and the three of them were very close. Dionni almost forgot she called Eva after she called Tiana because it took her so long to arrive.

"Is something wrong with Dior?" Eva questioned, motioning for the waitress to come over and take her order. Eva ran her fingers through her page boy hair cut and sat on the other side of Dionni.

Eva looked at Dionni's crestfallen face and thought, *What the hell could have happened that quick? Tears? There got to be something wrong with Dior.* Eva waited, looking into her friend's almost identical eyes. She again asked, "What's the matter, baby girl?"

Everywhere they went, Dionni and Eva were mistaken to be sisters. Eva was a little shorter and thicker than Dionni, but had the same skin tone and hazel eyes.

"Well, like I just telling T," Dionni said, shifting in her seat, "I had that meeting with Zay tonight, and I was feeling him just as much as I know that he was feeling me. But by the time I made it back to my car, I felt like I was cheating on Dale."

Dionni knew that she sounded so stupid, but if she couldn't confess her foolishness to her two best friends, then who could she run to?

"Girl," Eva sighed taking in a long breath, "you

scared the hell out of me. You making me want to beat you for even tripping over that fool Dale."

She looked across the table at Tiana and shook her head. "So, Zay is the guy that David was talking about?" Eva asked Tiana, attempting to be filled in.

She was in the shop getting a wash and blow dry when David called Tiana and gave them both a run down of his plans for Dionni. Both of the women thought it was a good idea, but looking at the expression on Dionni's face, now they were not too sure.

"You better quit crying because I can bet you all kinds of money that Dale is not any corner moaning and groaning over you," Tiana told Dionni. "You have been through so much with him, and if anyone understands what you are going through then it is definitely me, but like you told me, mama, you got to let it go."

"What happened with Zay that got you thinking like this anyway?" Eva asked, taking a sip from her drink.

Eva and Dionni became roommates after Tiana moved in with Rashied. At the time, Eva's new boo of the month was this guy named Mike. Mike kept telling Dionni that he had someone he wanted to hook her up with, but Dionni paid it no mind.

Because of Dionni's busy work and school schedule, she never was there when Dale was around. Dale seen a picture that Mike, Eva, and Dionni had taken and was blown away with Eva's girl. They both kept bugging Eva about Dionni, so she told them come by one night and waited till Dionni came home.

When Dionni walked in and saw Dale sitting on the couch, she was mad at herself for putting this meeting off. The brother was fine as hell. They went out for drinks afterwards and the rest is history.

*If I would have known that this shit was going to play out like this, then I would have never hooked them up,* Eva thought, shaking her head. She glanced back at Dionni, feeling so sorry for her.

"Like I told T, I think I like Zay," Dionni said playing with the emerald ring on her right ring finger. "I just feel like I am cheating on Dale. I haven't been with anyone else since I met Dale, and I really do not know how I should feel right now. I have been ducking and dodging Dale for the past couple of months, so I know he has to be getting the clear picture, but this time it is not on him. This shit is completely on me."

Dionni turned around and signaled the waitress to bring her another drink. She was on her fifth martini and was really starting to relax. She pushed her hair back out of her face and smiled after a quick thought came to her head. "I think I just need to see Dale one more time and tell him exactly how I feel.

Tiana and Eva looked at each other wondering what else they could do to help her get over this fool.

Eva broke the silence. "What is it going to take to get him out of your system? I thought you didn't care anymore. Are you bipolar now?"

Eva was trying to get a smile out of her friend, but Dionni was just staring at the people on the dance floor. Tiana and Eva wanted the best for their friend, but didn't know what could be done or said to eliminate all thoughts of Dale.

Dionni still did not say thing. Her thoughts were on Dale and the first night they met.

Tiana and Eva were still dumbstruck by the words that came from the lips of their friend. The three some just sat in silence and finished their drinks.

# Chapter 5

The next week went quickly for Zay. He flew to the South to witness his sister graduate from college and took her shopping in the Underground, a shopping center in Downtown Atlanta. He convinced Sasha to come home before she went on her graduation trip to Italy with some of her sorority sisters.

Sasha was kind of upset though, because during his entire stay in Atlanta she did not have her big brother's attention. Zay's phone kept ringing, and he was conducting business damn near his entire trip. She loved her brother like he was her daddy because technically he *was* the only father she knew. Zay was only six years older than her, but he did everything to make her happy.

She was impressed how he got his degree online while working in the streets trying to make sure that she was cool. She told herself that if her brother could get a college degree, so could she.

Sasha never knew *exactly* what Zay did for money, but she did know it was illegal. She felt the less she knew about it, the better. He always had some top notch chicks on his arm, but his main girl was Candy. She was the one who assisted Zay with raising Sasha and taught her how to conduct herself as a woman.

Candy was dark skinned and very beautiful. Her hair was always on point, and she carried herself like a model. She had body for days and stayed fly rocking all of the latest fashions. Sasha did not want to believe that Candy could do any wrong, but she knew looking deep into her eyes that she had another side of her that she kept hidden within herself.

Zay gave Candy the money, and she would take Sasha shopping for clothes and shoes. She taught her the importance of taking care of her body and her skin, and at all times to watch out for men.

"Because you got natural beauty, you don't have to try hard at all," she told her one day while arching her eyebrows. "Men are just going to flock after you."

She taught Sasha how to manage the thick curly manes that Sasha and her brother both inherited and explained to her that importance of remembering that beauty is not everything. Candy stressed to Sasha on a daily basis that she was going to go to college and get an education. "You are already beautiful," Candy would tell her. "Impress them a little more when you display intelligence as well."

For a long time, Sasha believed that Candy was Zay's girlfriend because she was around all the time. She wanted to know why he always had all these other women around and wouldn't marry her when he started to work as an investment banker.

After finally asking her brother the status of Candy and his relationship, Sasha was dumbstruck by his answer. He explained to her that Candy was *just* a close friend and business partner. When he met her they became cool, and Zay promised to look out for her at all times as long as she looked out for Sasha. She was more like another sister to him, and wanted Sasha to know how to conduct herself as a lady.

Between Candy and Zay, they made sure that Sasha had a normal teenage life and was proud that she was graduating from high school with no babies. When Sasha got accepted into college, Candy explained to her why she was so proud and gave her some advice while she was in college. "Baby girl, you make sure you finish school and get that paper," she told Sasha through tears the day Sasha left for Atlanta.

"I wish I was smart enough to go to school, and if it wasn't for your brother making sure that I stayed afloat, I don't know where I would be at today," Candy continued. "He made sure I was straight all these years, and I made sure you were as well. Don't go out there batting them thick eye lashes at them country ass niggas and come back pregnant, ok? You go out there and finish what you started, and hopefully I will still be here when you come back."

Sasha was confused on why Candy said she might be gone, but decided she would stay out of her business. As long as Candy was there for her, then there was nothing else she could ask for.

Candy stayed in touch with Sasha over the years. The pair was still close, but every time they spoke Candy was impressed on how fast Sasha was becoming independent and was being introduced to life on her own terms.

By this time, Candy moved to Los Angeles to establish their company out there. She still stayed on Sasha though, but it seemed to Sasha that the calls were not as frequent as they once were. Even though Sasha didn't like the sudden distance, she followed all of the advice that both Zay and Candy taught her, and soon she graduated.

While on the airplane back to Vegas, Sasha was still curious on where exactly Candy was. Zay told her when he first got to A-Town that she was out of the country, but that was so weird to Sasha. Candy, of all people, should have been there to see her graduate. She was there for *all* of the big events in Sasha's life that she could remember. Not saying anything else about it Sasha was hurt that Candy would miss such an important one.

The closer Zay and Sasha got to Vegas, the tenser Zay became. He kept fidgeting and glancing at his watch. He almost acted as if he was afraid of heights, but he'd flown too many times to count.

As soon as the plane touched down, he hurried and collected their luggage from baggage claim and whisked Sasha home. He informed her that he had plans for her and asked her to change into the outfit that he purchased her as a graduation present. Zay was taking her out for a night on the town to celebrate her accomplishments and stressed the fact that they could not be late.

Sasha was tired, but did as her brother commanded and went up stairs to get ready. She slipped on a crimson red strapless Jovani dress that stopped right above her knees. On her feet, she wore a pair of matching open toed two-inch heel sandals that strapped up her calves.

She had flat ironed her hair straight and it hung inches past her shoulders in a layered style. She wore no makeup and added just a touch of pink lip gloss to her lips for color. When she came down the stairs, Zay admired his baby and reached out to kiss her gently on the cheek.

"You are so beautiful," Zay told her, giving her another look over. "You ready to go?"

She smiled and said, "Yeah, big bro, I'm ready, and might I add, you looking mighty dapper yourself. I thought you only wore the ostrich when it was a special occasion."

Zay had on a tan pair of ostrich boots to go with a sable brown Armani Exchange set she had never seen before. He had his hair in his typical tight chain ponytail and had a fresh goatee. On his wrist, he wore a gold Jacob's original, and a gold diamond encrusted cross hung from around his neck.

"Dang, man, you doing it big like this?" she said while popping his collar. I guess I should graduate from college more often because I sure am impressed."

Zay smiled but tried to hide the apprehension he had in hopes of everything going well tonight. Zay was a hands on individual, but because of the short notice had to leave everything up to Dionni.

Dionni kept Zay updated by pictures she sent by text message from her blackberry, but Zay was still nervous. The presentation so far was lovely, but still he was nervous. He wanted everything to be perfect for his sister and hoped that this fine ass thick chick he was paying really had her shit together.

Since Zay left Dionni back at Olives, he couldn't stop thinking about her. He was glad he hired her because that had been his excuse for blowing her phone up. He knew the constant phone usage was aggravating to Sasha, but when she saw what he had in store for her, she would quickly forgive him for all of his trouble.

The only information he had for the event was that it was hosted at the Palazzo Hotel and Resort. Dionni informed him that for all of services she had included in the party sponsored by the hotel, the events coordinator was throwing in a two-night stay for Sasha which included a spa package. Again, Zay was impressed, but still yearned to see the final product himself.

When Zay turned the Range Rover into the sophisticated entrance of the hotel, Sasha's eyes widened. This hotel was not around when she left for school and being a native of Vegas, she rarely ventured to the strip, but she was impressed by the aurora of prestige that the hotel was releasing. Zay valet the car and took the hand of his sister to lead her to the club.

"This shit is hot, Zay," Sasha told her brother. "Ain't this where Jay-Z's Club 40/40 is located?" she asked. Zay nodded yes and hurried up his pace to the entrance of the Lavo Night Club. There was a line wrapped around the club and Sasha began to notice that there were a lot of people there that looked so familiar to her. "Damn, Zay, this is a class reunion," she said and tried to stop to speak to a chick she went to high school with.

Zay kept a firm grip on her hand and gently pulled her to the entrance. Sasha turned to smile at the girl and motioned with her lips that she was going to get at her once inside. Zay shook his head at Sasha, noticing he was upsetting her by the way her lip was starting to poke.

"You a rude motherfucker," she mumbled under her breath, upset that her brother was still treating her like a child.

Once inside the club, Sasha's frustrations slowly evaporated from the ambiance of the club. The theme of the club was classy and contemporary, and it was crowded. While Sasha continued to look around, Zay nodded his head toward the dj booth. The music suddenly stopped and the club suddenly fell quiet. After a few moments, a woman's voice came across the air waves.

"Greetings everyone," the voice started off. "I would like to ask Zay and Sasha to come to the booth, please." Sasha looked at her brother, wondering what exactly did have up his sleeves. Zay led her through the crowd to the booth, and the owner of the mysterious voice approached them.

Sasha gave the woman a once over, curious of what was going on. She wore a grey Versace dress that stopped right above the knees. She appeared confident and elegant.

*She's cute*, Sasha thought, wondering how her brother felt about this mystery woman.

Smiling, Dionni handed Zay the microphone and he turned to the crowd. "What's up, everyone," he began, periodically glancing at his sister. "I am Zay, and I am the one who asked all of you to come here tonight. You all know that Sasha just graduated from college, and I wanted you all to come out and show her your love and congratulate her personally." Sasha began to tear up. "Shardai, Danielle, Olivia, and Deisha, can you please come up here?" Zay spoke into the mic while looking into the crowd. Sasha's sorority sisters appeared out of nowhere and Sasha screamed, hugging them. She was not supposed to meet back up with them until next week to fly to Italy. Sasha could not believe that once again her brother did his thing and looked out for her.

"Dude, how did you do this?" she said between tears, glancing up at Zay.

He responded by saying, "My girl right here did everything. I did what I do best and was the financial advisor."

Zay introduced Dionni to Sasha. The ladies embraced, and Sasha excused herself to go mingle with her friends.

"When you are ready to dip out," Zay said, "go to the front desk and get your key. Dionni hooked you up to stay here for two days and enjoy a spa package. Happy graduation, baby, I am so proud of you." He kissed her on the cheek.

Sasha thanked them again and started to dance off into the crowd. She abruptly turned around and asked Zay, "Where's Candy? She's not here either?"

Zay was caught off guard by her question. He believed the answer he gave her in Atlanta about Candy was going to suffice, but by the curious look on his sister's face he was definitely mistaken.

"I told you she was out of the country on business," he replied. "She really wanted to make it tonight. Don't let that mess up your night. She will be here before you leave on your trip. I promise. Go have fun, girl. All of these folks are here for you."

Slowly, Sasha disappeared into the crowd and tried to enjoy herself. She was disappointed no doubt because for as long as she could remember Zay and Candy had been her only backbone. She was starting to get upset, but told herself fuck it. At that moment she spotted Jared, this guy she had a crush on almost her entire high school experience. She couldn't believe he was here for her. She heard that he was playing ball overseas so for him to be here was real cool. She brushed that Candy shit off her shoulders and turned her attention to Jared.

Zay was watching the entire scene from the dj booth and let out a sigh of relief. He knew eventually Sasha was going to bring Candy up again, but he did not think about it for tonight. Turning to Dionni, Zay said softly, "Thank you for real. This shit is hot and I can't believe you did all of this by yourself. I was nervous as hell, but David assured me that you would come through."

At that moment, TI's "Whateva You Like" came on and they both burst out laughing. "I guess that speaks for itself," Dionni said and the pair started to dance to the music. Everything turned out perfect, and for the rest of the night they continued to enjoy each other's company.

# Chapter 6

Dale was still coming on strong, but Dionni kept ignoring all of his efforts while donating her free time to Zay. They went to shows, lounges, and the movies together. He constantly was sending her flowers and gifts to her office and home whenever he was away on business, which made her feel like a young girl experiencing her first crush. She believed that what allowed them to get along so well was the fact they both had hectic work schedules. So, when they were together they were *together*. In spite of the sweetness, there was something in the back of her head that kept telling her not to get too close.

She understood why she was feeling skeptical, especially after what happened the other night. At Sasha's party, she didn't say anything about the conversation she heard between Zay and Sasha. She noticed how uncomfortable Zay became when his sister brought up Candy. This made Dionni certain that there was more information behind *that* situation. Overall, Zay had been the ideal man to Dionni, but shit, so was everyone one of them fools when the dating process first started off.

She liked the fact that Zay understood she was not ready to have sex. She briefly explained to him what happened with Dale and how he cheated on her for the majority of their relationship.

Dionni didn't want to make that mistake again.

Zay told her that he understood where she was coming from and never overstepped his boundaries. She was really starting to let Zay get under her skin. She liked him and Dionni decided that she was going to show him just how much. They returned to his house after attending the George Wallace Show at the Flamingo and were wrapped up in each other's arms on his sofa. Dionni laid her head onto his chest.

"Zay, you know that I am digging you, right?" she started off while slowly running her fingertips up and down his side. He tensed up by the sensations that were shooting through his body.

Since day one, he knew that Dionni was all that he wanted, but wasn't quite sure how exactly she felt about him. He knew he was making her happy by the way they spent so much time together, but other than that he was lost. There were times when they were together, and he was convinced he was all that she wanted and needed, but then there were also times when he was sure her mind was elsewhere. Those were the times that he was unsure of the status of their relationship.

Dionni kissed Zay's chest through his shirt and looked up into his eyes.

"Did you hear me?" she asked him while reaching up to kiss him on his neck. By this time, Zay's breathing sped up a bit but he tried to appear cool.

"Yes, ma'am," he said slowly. "What's on your mind?"

Dionni continued to run butterfly kisses across his neck. She unbuttoned his shirt and gracefully traced wet kisses back down his now bare chest.

She stopped above his belly button and looked up intensely into his questioning eyes. She stared at him long and hard.

After another brief silence, Dionni started speaking again. "Babe, I am really digging you. I know I don't show my emotions too much, and that is only because I don't want to be hurt again. Can you feel where I am coming from?"

She glided her body further down his legs until her breast rested on top of his knees. She never took her eyes off of him hoping that she could read the emotions through his eyes.

Zay tried to keep his composure, but it was hard for him to think. The way that Dionni was acting was brand new to him. He had tried to be a gentleman throughout their entire relationship, but God knew how many times he dreamt about how her honey pot was going to feel on top of his well endowed tool.

Dionni knew she had his mind going crazy and she was enjoying every moment of it. She slowly took his trembling right hand and kissed each finger one by one. Slowly she sucked on the tips and then ran her tongue down to the base of his hand. While doing all of this, she continued to stare into his eyes.

"Baby, why are you shaking? What's wrong?" she asked him, stopping abruptly midway down the shaft of his middle finger. "Do you want me to stop?" She tried to look as innocent as she could.

Zay couldn't concentrate. Majority of the time, he had complete control of the situation, but Dionni was the leader in this round. His head was resting back on the arm of his sofa while his eyes were completely shut. He was hoping that she would continue her journey further down south, and the next shaft she would be going down was his dick.

It took a moment for him to realize she stopped. He shook his head and replied, "What, baby? What did you say? I, I didn't hear you." Embarrassed for being caught off guard, Zay reached down and pulled Dionni toward him. Attempting to take over the situation, he cupped her face between his hands and kissed her as softly as he could. "You have my undivided attention. What did you say?" He kissed her again, this time separating her lips with his tongue, seductively making love to her mouth.

For a moment Dionni was lost in translation, temporarily forgetting what she asked him herself.

Not wanting to be upstaged, Dionni pulled herself together and broke the kiss. She quickly got up and walked out of the room.

A confused Zay stayed planted on the couch. He did not understand what was going on and called for her to come back. The first time, she did not answer so he called her name again.

"Dion--" Zay started to yell her name again as she emerged carrying a bottle of White Zinfandel and a glass of ice. "Damn, girl, how you know I didn't want anything?" he started off as she placed the glass and the bottle onto the table.

Ignoring his question, Dionni wiggled out of the form fitting skinny jeans she was wearing and slid off her blouse. Throwing the clothing articles onto the couch, Dionni looked down at Zay and smiled. She watched his face trying to figure out exactly what he was thinking. Knowing she got his attention, her smile turned to a smirk. She turned her back to him, wanting him to see how firm and inviting her body appeared wearing only a sheer yellow bra and matching thong.

She picked her props up off the table and placed her almost naked body down onto the rug in the middle of his floor. She opened her legs and pulled the material of her thong to the side. She spread her full lips apart with her left hand and licked her first three fingers of the right. Slowly she inserted each of her fingers into her wetness one at a time never taking her eyes off of Zay.

Next, she removed a cube of the melting ice from the glass, rubbing her clitoris with it until it began to swell. Zay was frozen in the same spot on the couch with a look of shock and pleasure on his handsome face. He appeared to be enjoying himself, but was apprehensive on what he should do next.

Dionni continued to please herself with the ice for a moment longer until it melted completely from the warmth of her juices. She took a swig from the Zinfandel bottle and softly asked, "Would you like some?" A smile appeared on Zay's face as he slid off of the couch and crawled to join Dionni on the rug.

Dropping his shirt on the floor, he removed his own piece of ice from the glass. He hesitated for a moment, and then ran the ice down the fullness of her already wet lower lips. A seductive moan escaped her lips and it was Dionni's turn to throw her head back in enjoyment while she clutched each of her full breasts.

Zay placed the ice into his mouth. He grabbed Dionni by the waist and firmly pulled her toward him. It was his turn to separate her pussy lips and licked inside of her walls exposing the coldness of his tongue. He then pushed the ice into her wetness with his tongue and smoothly sucked it out.

Going out of her mind, Dionni took the bottle of wine and drizzled it down her body until it met Zay's lip. Never skipping a beat, he continued on with this routine over and over until the ice was completely melted. He swallowed all of her sweet nectar that the combination of ice, wine, and her juices created.

Clenching the edges of the rug, Dionni releasing more than just moans from her body. She released all of the hurt that Dale had put upon her, she released all of the hate that she had for Ashley and the other bitches in Dale's life, and lastly, she released the growing emotions that she was holding back from Zay.

With her eyes firmly shut, she wrapped her bronze thighs around his neck until she almost suffocated him.

"Damn, baby, shit," she exclaimed, regaining consciousness. "Please make love to me, Zay, please," she begged him in almost a whisper. Zay couldn't believe this moment was finally here. Continuing to suck on her clit, Zay gently removed the bear hug that Dionni had on him with her legs, separating them into a V position. He slowly and softly trailed wet kisses down her left thigh until he reached her ankle, and repeated the action on her right.

"Play with that pussy," he commanded her as he removed his clothing from his bottom half. Obeying his request, Dionni rubbed and fingered herself wildly with anticipation. She was long overdue for whatever it was she was about to endure, and she knew he was ready to give it to her.

Zay bent down to give her a kiss, but was interrupted by the sound of click click click. The top lock of the front door was unlocked. Zay tensed up and turned to the direction of the door. Trying to cover Dionni's nakedness with his shirt and get up at the same time, Zay heard the bottom lock unlock and a tall, slender, chocolate frame walked in.

Dionni didn't know what to do. She was frozen in her spot. Even though she was damn near naked, Dionni couldn't take her eyes off of this mystery lady. She wanted to know if this was the infamous Candy. This chick just stood there glaring down at Dionni.

Dressed in all black, she had a classy aura about her, but had the appearance of a hood bitch written all over her face. She was rocking a short quick weave and had small facial features, but was thick as shit. She reminded Dionni of Delicious from *The Flavor of Love*, dressed in a strapless dress and thigh high black stiletto boots.

A thick cloud of awkwardness hung over the room engulfing the three of them. The woman stopped watching Dionni and turned her attention to Zay.

"Hey, ugh, I apologize, if I interrupted anything," she said. "I know I was not supposed to be here till next week, but I sealed the deal early, and wanted to surprise you with the bonus package."

She returned her attention to Dionni. "Um, hello," she said, "my name is Candice, but everyone calls me Candy. You must be Dionni, I have heard nothing but good shit about you," she continued, now gazing at the floor.

The polite thing would have been to over to Dionni and shake her hand, but by her degree of nakedness, she just stood rooted in her spot by the door. Zay walked over to the hall closet and retrieved a blanket and passed it to Dionni. Dionni was shocked by the entire situation that was transpiring before her eyes.

*I must be getting punk'd*, she thought while wrapping herself up into the blanket and standing. She was even more shocked that during this uncomfortable duration, Zay did not say one single word *and* this negro was still asshole naked.

Now that she was somewhat covered, Dionni answered Candy but kept her eyes on Zay. "Well, Candy, I am so happy that you know about me, but I really can not say the same thing about you. In fact, Zay, who the fuck is she?" she asked Zay, not knowing if she should laugh or scream.

"D, um, this is my business associate Candy," Zay said, attempting to keep an even tone while walking to retrieve his clothes. "She was in Chicago on business and I wasn't expecting her for a week, but who can cry 'bout spilled milk when there was money made in the process." Zay reached down and pulled on his pants.

This entire scene was fucking with Dionni because she was experiencing déjà vu. She felt like Ashley must have when she discovered her in the garage months back. She had never been on this side of the situation. She was the one who embarrassed the rats by walking in while they were in a compromising position, but never could anyone tell her that she would be the one caught literally with her legs wide open.

Candy brushed past them and retreated up the stairs to wherever she was going, hollering down the stairs, "Nice to meet you."

Zay's secretive demeanor was pissing Dionni off, and once the coast was clear she stood and pulled on her clothes.

"Man, this is some crazy shit," she muttered under her breath. *Dale never had any female living with him and acting like it was all cool and shit.*

"Baby, it is not like that. She stays here when she is in town, but she lives in Cali. I promise I wouldn't disrespect you like that. She practically helped me raise

Sasha. I don't have any reason to lie to you. Never have we been intimate before. She is just a good friend, and in the end, we began making money together. Please don't look like that."

He tried to reassure Dionni. Dionni tried to be optimistic, but something in the back of her head kept telling her to just be careful. She assured Zay that everything was okay and went home leaving the issue alone.

# Chapter 7

"Can I get a Venti Carmel Frapachino with extra caramel and extra whip cream?" Dionni asked the attendant at the Starbucks drive thru. Dionni and Dior were out cruising the streets after a morning at the groomers. Dionni paid the attendant as Dior bounced onto her lap, rocking her cute little bow at the ears.

"Awe, she is so adorable," the attendant told Dionni.

"Thank you, sweetie," she replied, taking her drink. "Can I get a puppy cream for her as well?"

"Sure," she said and went back to retrieve the puppy treat. Dionni sat back and turned up her radio.

A song she had never heard before came on by one of her favorite neo soul singers. In "Another Again," John Legend sang about breaking up, swearing off his girl only to get back together again. She rubbed her puppy and shook her head, "Damn, Dior, this song is me and Dale. I can't believe that I went through that shit all those times."

The Starbucks attendant gave Dionni the cream for Dior, and Dionni pulled off slowly thinking about her relationships old and new. The last three months with

Zay went by so quickly and she was confused on how she was feeling. She was really digging him and he officially became her honey, but she was still missing Dale.

Thinking back to that day that she discovered Ashley in the garage was making Dionni upset all over again and she turned the radio to a gospel station in hopes that the praise music would remove the demon that was sitting on her chest. She tried to think positive thoughts while she continued to drive down the street, but Dionni kept hearing Zay's voice in her head.

Zay acted as if nothing happened and had not said anything else about Candy. It had been a week since the incident with Candy, but Dionni felt like it just happened yesterday. Dionni wanted to tell him that she didn't feel too comfortable with Candy having a key to his house, but tried not to make a big deal out of it. Candy had been in the picture long before her, and could no man tell her not to be cool with David, so Dionni decided to enjoy her time with Zay and not expect anything from him. All she wanted out of it was not to be hurt, and she convinced herself that she was going to enjoy the ride Zay gave her till the wheels fell off. Even if she couldn't enjoy Zay's ride that night due to the rude interruption by.

Her cell phone rang and Zay's face appeared on her screen.

"Hey, baby," she crooned into the phone, "what's up?"

"I haven't heard the music of your voice all day, just had to check up on my lil' mama. What you been up to, sexy?"

She blushed. She loved the sound of his voice over the phone and loved how he called her lil' mama.

"Oh, nothing, baby, just got Dior all hooked up at the groomers and on my way home. I'm 'bout to stop at the store real quick to get her some food first. What's on your agenda for later on, have I been penciled in somewhere?"

She could hear the smile on his face as he responded, "You know it. Just get at me when you two make it home. Maybe, we can get a couple of movies and takeout, and make it a blockbuster night. How that sound, baby?"

Dionni smiled from ear to ear, forgetting that just a couple of moments ago she was in limbo about their relationship. "Papi, you know whatever it is that you want to do, that is fine with me."

"Well alright then," he replied. "Get at me when you make it home."

Dionni pulled into the neighborhood pet supply store and put Dior on her leash. While checking out what new vitamins were out for puppies, Dionni did not notice someone was watching her.

Dale noticed her when she pulled up, but was indecisive if he should leave or stay. Dionni had been on his mind for awhile, and he was thanking God for answering his prayers. He knew that she was a frequent flier of the store and came here periodically to see if he could catch a glance of her. She had been avoiding his ass for real, and he was unsure of what was going to happen.

Dionni was deep in thought when Dale approached her slowly down the aisle. He tried to remain cool and not show how anxious he was to see her. He knew that if she still cared about him, it was going to be hard for her to stay mad at him with him in her face. Dionni had always been the type of person to let things go after awhile.

He knew that he was going to be hard to resist, today especially because he knew his appearance was right on point. He was rocking a fitted Black Label shirt with eagle wings on the back in gold and matching jeans. He was freshly lined from the barber shop and had on the cologne that she bought him, Issey Miyake.

Dionni noticed him as he got closer and she tried to act as if she did not see him at all. She felt his eyes on her as she spoke quietly to Dior and tried to regain her composure. She placed Dior down on the ground and pulled her short ass skirt down. She had worked hard to stay away from Dale, but he finally caught up with her.

Turning to face him, she casually said, "Hello," smiled, and walked past his fine ass.

*Damn he smells wonderful,* she thought and started to sway those magical hips of hers a little bit stronger as she made her way to the register.

"Hello," he said back, but seconds too late because he was lost watching her hips as she walked away. He saw her get out of her car in the parking lot, but didn't know that she would appear to be more beautiful up close and all of the feelings that he had tried to hide shown all over his face. He had always been in awe of her appearance, but today he was lusting behind her for real. He glanced down at those thick ass legs and he started to go back down memory lane. She had the most athletic legs that he had seen with small muscles bulging at the calves. She wasn't muscular though, but he knew that it was from all of those years that she had been wearing her sexy ass high heel shoes.

She had on white flip flops with a fresh French manicure on her toes. She rocked a white wife beater with the smallest skirt that he had ever seen her in or could remember.

"Damn, this girl is still bad as a motherfucka," he said to himself as she turned around and smiled back at him, this time giving him a full smile. He knew that he had to get his shit together because he would go crazy if there was another man hugging, kissing, or admiring his girl.

She appeared to be a teenager with the loose ponytail that she was sporting, but by looking into her eyes, anyone could tell that she was all woman.

"Hold on, sweetie," he said, bending down to give Dior a treat and pick her up. "How you doing?" he asked her, rubbing the puppy's head. "You look...nice today," he stumbled out trying to start a conversation.

Over the past couple of months, Dionni had been so cold toward him that now that she was in front of him giving him her undivided attention, he was at a loss for words. Usually Dale was "Mr. Rico Suave" and cocky as hell, but today he had a different vibe coming from him.

He looked deep into Dionni's eyes and was trying to read her emotions. He wanted to make love to her so badly and decided that he had to put his plan of getting her back into full effect before it was too late.

Dionni felt so uncomfortable because "Sexy" was suddenly awakened by his presence and was getting wetter and wetter by the moment. She could not believe that he still had this effect on her after all this time, and was trying to make herself get the hell up out of dodge.

"It was nice seeing you," she told Dale, breaking the silence between them. She removed Dior from his arms and went to pay for her merchandise.

Everything was in a blur to him after that, and as soon as she appeared in the store was how fast she vanished into her car.

When she was in the safety of her vehicle, Dionni took in a deep breath. She could not believe that he still had a hold over her like that and was not enjoying how she was feeling. She wanted so much to try to make things work with Zay, but just the mere presence of Dale made her weak and she did not like that. Getting herself together, she backed out of the parking lot and went home to where her new man would be momentarily.

"How much money did you deposit into my account?" Zay asked into the telephone while patting his body dry. He was getting ready to spend some time with Dionni but wanted to make sure business was going well to prevent having any interruptions. He knew the other night was still bothering Dionni and did not know exactly how to discuss it. He was hoping she would not bring it up.

"I put $10,000 in there and kept $2,500 for myself. I know you said I could keep three, but it is ok," Candy said. "You showed me love last time with the $5,000, so I can't be greedy. By the way, I am sorry again about walking in on you the other night. Usually you do not bring your women to the spot, so I did not expect to see what I did. She's cute though. Do you think it is going to work out between the two of you?"

"Man, I want it to work," he told her, stepping into his boxers, "but it is not going to work with you popping up without telling me. She is different from the rest, so I am coming at her from a different approach. She doesn't know shit about what is going on in our situation, and I respect how she feels and her opinions of me. Now I am going to have to explain why my so called business associate has a key and a room at my house."

Candy paused for a moment and finally responded, "You are right, I won't do it again." She tried to remain composed, but she was hurt by what he was saying. "Well, as long as you are happy, that is all that matters." She took a deep breath and excused herself from the conversation. "Go 'head and get at me later," she added, trying to hurry up and get off the phone.

"Aight then, ma," Zay replied back. "Peace."

Tears came to Candy's eyes as she hung up the phone. All of these years of dedicating herself to this man and doing everything that he may request and that meant *everything,* she could not believe he didn't see how much she wanted to be with him. Candy began to sob harder as thoughts came back to her of the night that Sasha left for college.

After leaving the airport, Zay quickly dropped her off and told her he had an appointment and would return to the house shortly. She went upstairs and changed into something comfortable and sulked for a moment. She missed Sasha so much already and knew that she had to tell Zay how she felt about him and quick. Candy got herself together and went downstairs to Zay's state of the art kitchen and prepared herself a Caesar salad.

Candy couldn't get the conversation that she and Zay had in the car out of her head. They discussed previously that after Sasha left, he wanted her to move to LA to his loft and conduct business from there. He informed her that it was time to branch out and it would be better for them in the long run.

Sitting alone in the kitchen lost in thought about how was going to disperse this plan, Candy heard the garage door open. "I hope this nigga is alone," she said while hurrying to finish her salad. She was not in the mood to entertain and it was apparent by her attire, a throwback football jersey and her hair wrapped in a scarf.

"Candy, this is Sophia," Zay told her after noticing her in the kitchen. He walked in with his arms wrapped around this damn near white broad that she had never seen before. Sophia had very strong, exotic features and a head full of curly red hair. Candy couldn't tell what she was mixed with, but at the moment she really could care less. "Sophia, this is Candy, my business associate."

Sophia smiled at Candy and extended a hand for her to shake. Candy, ignoring the gesture, gave her a head nod, picked up her salad, and started up the stairs.

"We didn't mean to interrupt you," Zay slurred to Candy, patting her on the ass as she walked by.

"Naw, you cool, this your house. I'm just a visitor," she replied back ignoring his gesture as well. Candy was really not in the mood for Zay's drunk ass at the moment, and all thoughts of telling him how she felt quickly rushed from her head.

Lying alone in the bed, Candy thought it might be a good idea for her to move to Cali. "This nigga ain't going to be right," she told herself.

"Candy." She thought she heard Zay call her name, but wasn't sure.

"Damn, bitch, you tripping for real, hearing this nigga voice and shit," she said shaking her head at the thought. She hoped he wasn't calling her anyway because she was not in the mood to see him entertain his guest in front of her face.

It was mind blowing to her that after all of these years, he couldn't see that she had feelings for him. Even though she never just came out and confessed her feelings to him, she knew Zay was not a dumb man. She couldn't understand why he played dumb to her emotions. She was in love with Zay and was determined to figure out how she…

"Candy."

Her thoughts were interrupted by Zay's voice outside her door. "Can you come here? I need to discuss something with you."

"Ok," she replied, shaking her thoughts off. "Give me one moment."

Candy's heart fluttered as she jumped up and decided that this was going to be the time that she let him know where he stood in her heart. His company must have left because whenever he was occupied, she had to remain out of sight, which meant out of mind. Candy got up and put on her robe.

Once outside of her door, she heard R Kelly's "Bump and Grind" coming from his room and this instantly made Candy wet. A million things were going through her head as she slowly made her way down the hallway to the bedroom of her employer and secret love of her life. When she reached his door, she tapped lightly.

"Come in," she heard him call out softly, which hardened the mounds on her breast.

*Maybe he is thinking the same thing*, she thought as she opened the door with sweaty hands.

Nervous about what was going to happen next, but excited at the same time, Candy entered Zay's dark abode. Her eyes had to adjust to the light as she closed the door behind her. Zay was lying across his bed with only a pair of off white silk pajama pants covering his lower half. Candy thought he was oh-so sexy by the way his long wavy hair hung around his face and down his back like Jesus' did.

"What's wrong, ma? Why do you look scared?" he asked her, noticing her sudden nervousness. "Come closer, I got something to ask you."

Gripping the tie of her robe with her left hand, Candy was trying to build up the courage to loosen it and display her chocolate naked body from beneath.

*He is waiting for you to move*, she thought, trying to convince herself that he wanted her just as bad as she wanted him. Her pussy was leaking in between her legs in anticipation of what was going to happen next. Zay was gazing at Candy so intensely, which made Candy pick up her pace.

Discovering that they were not alone, Candy stopped in her tracks as she turned her attention to the sound coming from his adjoining bathroom. Really confused by what was going on, Candy turned her attention back to Zay and asked him, "Is someone in there?"

Answering her question, the bathroom door opened and out walked the chick that was with Zay earlier that night. The stranger was asshole naked and stood in the doorway with her hands on her hips and a soft smirk on her lips. The hair on her pussy was cut into a triangle, and was just as red as the hair on her head.

Candy turned her attention back to Zay, noticing that he too had a smile on his face.

"Zay," Candy started off trying not to smack the grin off of his face. While she had her attention on Zay, she did not notice Sophia walk up behind her until she felt a tug on her robe tie. She turned her attention back to this bitch, trying to convince herself that this wasn't really happening.

Zay quickly got off the bed and stood behind her. Sophia still had a grip on her tie and released it from Candy's body.

"Damn, you're beautiful," Sophia said and leaned in to kiss her. Candy was frozen on site. This shit was happening too fast.

Candy tried to step back and cover her naked body, but forgot that Zay was in the room too. He rushed behind her and stood as a barricade. "Zay, what is going on..." she started again, this time interrupted by his hands rubbing and gripping her breasts.

Candy didn't know what to do. The sensation that ran through her body made the wetness between her legs reinstate, but never in a million years did she imagine the first time that they would share a sexual experience that it would happen like this.

"Kiss her back," Zay softly ordered Candy, pinching her hardening nipples with his right hand and moving down to the treasure between her legs with his left.

"She admired you from downstairs and she wanted to taste you." He said this to Candy in such a calm manner, like he just told her the time or the weather. He was grinding his dick against her ass, and Candy lost sight of the situation. The only thing she could attempt to focus on was the way it was going to feel when that monster entered her, and she began to leak even more.

Candy couldn't think because of the way Zay was finger fucking her. He had her body and mind all fucked up. Her breathing became distorted and Sophia leaned in again, this time licking the fullness of Candy's lips with her tongue. Then, slowly she entered Candy's mouth.

*If this is what he wants, then I guess I have no choice*, Candy thought.

Candy tried to go with the flow and relax herself, but could not make herself enjoy this situation. Sophia now took over rubbing her titties and was running her tongue down her body until she got to her pussy. Zay, never missing a beat, guided the pair to the bed.

Sophia only stopped what she was doing to allow Candy to lay on the bed. She pushed Candy's legs into the air, separating them at the same time. Her breathing became intensified and irregular as she licked three of her fingers and slowly pushed them into Candy.

Once she had a rhythm created, she started to lick Candy's clit, occasionally slurping and sucking.

Candy took in a deep breath to withstand the pressure of the hand fucking that she was enduring.

*If this is what Zay wants, then quit tripping*, she told herself while trying to display some really genuine fuck faces to Zay as he continued to watch the pair intensely.

"Grab her head," Zay ordered her again, and as always, she quickly obliged. "Run your fingers through her hair," he said while he dropped his pants to the floor, rubbing the head of his dick up and down Sophia's ass. The entire time he never took his eyes off of Candy. He watched the show in front of him for a few more moments before Sophia lifted her head and asked him to taste her.

He got on his knees and began to eat the shit out of Sophia's pussy. Candy let go of the grip that she had on Sophia and turned her own head to the side. She could not believe that she let herself get into this situation. While Sophia was trying to hang with Zay, Candy was laying there emotionless while this bitch continued to lick, spit, nibble, and caress on her pussy.

Sophia couldn't take anymore and finally started to moan, "Please fuck me, Daddy, please." Zay continued on for a few more moments before he stopped to reach over and grab the already open pack of condoms off of the dresser. While he was doing this, Sophia climbed on top of Candy and started to kiss her passionately. Candy did not want to kiss her again, but didn't want to throw off the groove that Zay was in. She pretended to enjoy the kiss that she was sharing with Sophia, occasionally pausing to nibble and suck on her bottom lip.

Zay licked his lips and after securing the condom, he paused in debates of which one of these beautiful creatures that he was going to penetrate.

It didn't take him long to decide though, and shoved himself into Sophia while she remained doggy style over Candy. He started to bang the shit out of her pussy holding onto her hips while talking shit to them at the same time. "Bitch, you like this dick? I said, do you like this dick?" He must have been talking to Sophia because she was the one he was seductively driving his tool into, but while doing so, he stared Candy dead in her eyes.

"Scoot down so you can put her pretty ass titties in your mouth," he demanded Candy. He reached down and started to pull her leg downward to hang more off of the bed.

*He must be trying to hurry up and cum so that he can handle me*, she thought as she slid her body down the bed.

"Wrap your legs round me," he told her while continuing to drive his dick into Sophia. Again, she followed the directions that were given to her, sucking Sophia's titties and wrapping her long legs around Zay's ass. She placed her wetness directly onto the bottom section of his shaft and his balls.

Even though Zay could not physically see exactly what Candy was doing, he knew that he was really feeling it by how Sophia couldn't control herself. She was being double teamed for real and came all over herself so many times that she could not even keep up count. Candy knew that this had to be a sight though, because if someone walked in, they might think this nigga was fucking both of them at the same time.

Zay couldn't hold on anymore and had to cum. Feeling Zay gyrate and shake against her G-spot made Candy cum as well. Removing himself from the grip that both of these women had on him, Zay crashed on the opposite side of the bed away from the duo.

Candy rolled over onto her side and waited, knowing that after what just went down, it would soon be her turn.

"He wants me so badly," she whispered to herself, pinching her own nipples and smirking to herself. *He only came because he felt me on him and watched my every move.*

She was so lost in her own thoughts she did not hear Zay address her again.

"Candy," Zay said, standing up and walking to the bathroom. "Thank you, ma, you can go back into your room now. Now that Sophia tasted you, we can have our round three, but that was some wild shit. You might need to initiate that with some of those folks in the street." He said all of this with his back to her as he released himself from the condom and washed himself in the sink.

"Ain't this some shit," Candy said out loud not giving a fuck if he heard her or not.

Realizing that tears were streaming from her eyes, Candy remembered that she was in the privacy of her own home. She was laying in her own bed, under her goose down comforter. Candy started to shudder. Every time she thought about that crazy ass night, she ended up in tears. Candy didn't know what exactly allowed Zay to have such a hold onto her.

After Zay displayed his *true* feelings for Candy, she decided that she is only going to stick around jut for the money. *Hell,* she got her own three bedroom beach front condo, a Cross Fire to drive, and can shop as much as she wanted. What else could she ask for?

Love…. But since she couldn't get it from Zay, she had to let it go. She kept in touch with Sasha, but had to remember that she was not her mother. It was still fucking with her that she missed Sasha's graduation, but she didn't want Zay to feel like he still had complete power of her.

It had been on her mind since the graduation wondering if he even cared. Did she cross his mind at all? He probably didn't lose not one bit of sleep, especially since he got that new red bone on his arm.

*Where did she come from anyway?* Candy thought to herself. *She's pretty and all, but damn! She ain't badder than me! He probably just fucking with her because of those funny looking eyes she got, and they probably contacts. SHIT!*

Candy shook it off and looked at the time. It was getting late and she had an early flight in the morning. Candy rolled over and tried to ward the nightmares away that were filled with Zay, Sophia, and his new bitch, Dionni.

# *Chapter 8*

It had been three months since Dionni and Zay started to have sex and they had grown so close during this time. Dionni was even half way living at Zay's house. In the beginning, she was uncomfortable going over there because she did not want *Candy* walking in on them again. She explained this to Zay, and with in the hour, he had his on call locksmith come over and re-key everything.

He assured her that Candy was *NOT* an issue. He emphasized the importance of Dionni in his life while placing a key into her hand, and told her that he really wanted their relationship to go further. Hesitant, Dionni didn't know if she should believe this, but told herself that if she could give *Dale* a chance, she d*amn* sure could give Zay one as well.

Dionni spent many nights over there, and just like Zay promised, she did not see or even hear about Candy. In the back of her mind, she questioned what happened to her, but was enjoying the time that they were sharing.

Between the two of them, they were both out of town a lot, so that made their time together even more special. Zay was in Detroit at a conference for financial advisors. He called her earlier in the day and explained to her that was missing her so much. He wanted for her to fly to out and spend a day or two with him.

At first, she explained to him that she wasn't going to be able to because she had proposals to prepare for three perspective clients, but he convinced her that she could take care of that there while he was gone during the day. She thought about it a couple more minutes and quickly chimed a, "Yes," over the phone only if Tiana or Eva agreed to look out for Dior.

By three that afternoon she was in the air on her way to Michigan, excited to see her man. She guessed he was happy to see her as well by his greeting for her when she exited the plane. She fell into his awaiting arms and he kissed her so passionately, Dionni was happy that she agreed to come.

They grabbed a quick bite to eat and went back to the hotel suite that had been Zay's new home for the past couple of days. Once settled on the couch, they filled each other in with all of the experiences they had since the last time they were in each other's presence while Zay massaged Dionni's tight shoulders.

"Baby, you need to relax," Zay told her, kissing the back of her neck. "I'm going to draw you a bath, bathe, and massage you in the water. How does that sound?" he crooned into her ear. He laid her back gently against the arm of couch and propped a pillow behind her head. He left her alone and went to the bathroom.

In the distance, Dionni could hear the running of the bath water and she closed her eyes. She was so happy that he convinced her to fly down and get away from reality. She had been taking on so many new clients and knew she had built up tension in her shoulders and neck. Her thoughts were interrupted when she heard Zay's footsteps approach her.

Zay gently pulled her onto her feet and started to undress her. He took his time as he unbuttoned her skirt and slid it carefully down her legs. Dionni felt the moisture between her legs begin as he massaged her thighs and her calves. Dionni remained silent as he continued to undress and massage her entire body. Once she was completely naked, Zay picked Dionni up and carried her into the bathroom as if she was a small child.

He placed her gracefully into the warm water and started to bathe her. Her bath lasted for about forty-five minutes as he washed her hair and lathered her entire body. Dionni was so relaxed and in a zone that she did not realize that he was finished. Zay stood her up and towel dried her body. Once completed, he again lifted her out of the bathroom and placed her onto the bed where he finished her massage.

Dionni must have fallen asleep because when she opened her eyes, it was completely dark in the bedroom. She was still naked but was covered by a thick, warm comforter, cuddling the hotel pillow. She glanced over to the clock sitting on the nightstand and saw that it was 3:32 am.

"Baby?" Dionni said, reaching over for Zay.

There was no response. The other side of the bed was empty and Dionni realized that she was alone.

"Zay!" Dionni called out into the darkness. She waited for another moment, and there still was not a response. *Where the hell is he?* she thought to herself. She attempted to call his name a couple more times before she decided to give him a call on his cell phone.

She dialed his number and waited for him to answer. *He must have run out to the store,* she thought to herself. The phone rang until his voicemail picked up.

"Babe, it's me," she started off. "I am just calling to see where did you sneak off to. I'm sorry that I went to sleep on you. Please give me a call if you are in a store. I think I want an iced tea."

Dionni hung up and stretched out in the bed. It had only been a couple of times that she has woken up back home and Zay was gone, but he always had a legitimate excuse such as running to the store or grabbing a bite to eat. But, this was not the 24 hr town of Las Vegas. They were in Detroit. *Do they even have 24 joints out here?* she thought to herself.

Not trying to let her emotions get the best of her, Dionni rolled over and went back to

sleep. When she reopened her eyes, it was 4:26 am. Zay still hadn't returned.

She glanced at down at her cell phone to see if she slept through his call. Dionni had no missed calls. She tried to call him again, and like before, no answer. She left another message and hung up.

Dionni hated feeling like this. When she was with Dale she had many sleepless nights like this. She hated how shit like this made her feel. Waking up every hour checking to see if he was there or calling his phone. No response. Turning over taking another cat nap, and waking up again thirty minutes to an hour later and he still hadn't returned. Calling his phone again, still no response. Repeating this cycle over and over until finally his phone was just going straight to voice mail.

She promised herself that she would not go through this again, and look at her now. She tried to go back to sleep, but could not. She laid there till 5:10 am and decided to try again. Just like she predicted, the phone was going straight to voicemail.

*If this fool is not here in the next hour, I am going home. What the hell was he thinking? I could have stayed at home for this shit! I thought he was missing me so damn much? I know I was tired and we didn't have sex, but damn! Leave and not answer the phone? He got me oh so fucked up.....*

Dionni got out of the bed and tried to find the light switch. She was trying to find her luggage but knew she couldn't do it completely in the dark. Once she turned on the lights, she located her bags and quickly got dressed into a velour sweat suit and brushed her hair into a ponytail. She put on her shoes and repacked her bags.

By this time, it was almost six o'clock. She picked up the telephone and attempted to call him again. The phone was still going straight to voice mail. She called the airlines and booked a flight that was going to leave by nine. She called the front desk and requested for a cab to come and pick her up.

The entire time she appeared so calm and collected, but deep down she was a mental wreck. Part of her was hoping that Zay would suddenly appear in the room or see her leaving in the lobby and she could just cancel everything. She wanted to cuss him out and he would explain where he was, but forty five passed, and the only phone that rang was the phone located in the suite informing Dionni that her cab was there.

She was going to leave Zay a note, but decided against it. *Did that negro leave me a something saying where the hell he was at!!!! Hell naw! And I don't want to hear that business shit because the only business that is conducted financially in the wee hours of the morning is between a man and a woman. Why the hell would he have me fly all the way down here? This shit is crazy.... I'm GONE.....*

Dionni got her things together and left the room. She went down the elevator and walked through the hotel lobby. The entire time she was hoping she would catch a glance of Zay, or he would at least call her on her G1 that she was carrying in her hand. She took one more look around the hotel lobby and got into her awaiting cab.

# Chapter 9

*Dionni is going to kill me,* Zay thought to himself when he turned off the power to his cell. Dionni had called three times and it was killing him not to answer, but if she knew that he was with Candy….. He couldn't even imagine what the hell would have happened. He was in the waiting room of the Detroit Memorial Hospital.

He had Candy fly down from California yesterday because he had a potential client that wanted to meet her. He knew that she was going to meet him for dinner, but he did not know that around midnight he would be receiving a call from the hospital.

Zay finished moisturizing Dionni's body with her shea butter lotion and was just about to wake her up so that he could taste her. He knew that he worked crazy hours, but so did his baby. He wanted her just to relax and let him take care of her.

That was a problem that he mentioned to her on so many occasions, so when Dionni just relaxed and let him pamper her, he wanted to make it last as long as he could. He guessed that is why she was so successful in her field. Dionni wanted her clients to be satisfied 100%

when it came to one of her events, and she worked many long and hard hours.

When she arrived in Detroit, he felt that she was just as happy to see him as he was her, but the stress that she has been experiencing was written all over her face. Zay wanted Dionni to relax while she was with him. He wanted the cares of the outside world to disappear from their lives and them to just enjoy each other.

When the hospital staff called and informed him that Candy was in the hospital, he thought that he would be gone long enough to pick Candy up and take her back to her room. Candy has been roughed up in the past by clients, but usually she was quick on her feet and could handle the situation.

Zay was not prepared to see Candy lying the in the hospital bed beaten. He barely recognized her! Her right eye was swollen shut, she had a long cut going across her forehead, and she had cuts and bruises all over her entire body.

The triage nurse informed him that she was repeatedly raped and may have internal bleeding. The doctor recommended for Candy to stay in the hospital for a couple of days for observation. He could not leave Candy alone like this! That would be so fucked up, but how the hell was he going to explain this to Dionni. He knew that he would eventually have to tell her the truth, but damn, he did not think that think it would be like this.

After several hours, Candy finally woke up. At first when she opened her eyes and seen Zay, a faint smile appeared on her face but quickly disappeared. She turned her head in the direction of the window and took a few moments to speak.

"Where's Dionni?" she faintly asked him in almost a whisper.

"I'm, uh uh, I'm not sure," he stammered, embarrassed by his answer. He was not lying. He really did not know where Dionni was. He checked his messages and listened to the two that she left, but that was it.

Zay was feeling like shit right now because Dionni had explained to him time and time again how badly Dale has hurt her with his childish antics, and he assured her on more than one occasion that he was the exact opposite. But was he? If the shoe was on the other foot, Zay would have been mad as hell.

"What do you mean your not sure?" Candy asked, interrupting his thoughts. "I thought you said she was here, so I should only call you if it is an emergency." She still spoke in a soft voice, but her tone seemed like a mocking type. "I wasn't going to call you, but I felt that this was kind of important, don't you think?"

Tears ran down Candy's face as she spoke, and Zay was hurting for her. He knew that Candy loved him, and he loved her as well, but not like she wanted him to. Candy did any and everything that Zay asked for, but that was the problem. She did not have a mind of her own. He wanted a woman to wife, not be his puppet. Every time Candy mentioned or hinted that they should be together, Zay would ignore it entirely.

In all of the years that Zay had known Candy though, he had *NEVER* seen her cry. She always had her game face, so to see her break down was crazy to him. *Damn, this girl must be in pain,* Zay thought to himself. The only thing was Zay wasn't sure if she was in pain from the attack or from everything that he had put her through.

"Candy, what happened?" Zay asked her, rubbing her hair out of her face.

Candy turned and looked up into Zay's eyes. No words came out of her mouth, but the pain that projected from her eyes explained to him that she was not ready to speak about it.

The tears streamed from her face, and she turned her attention back to the window.

Zay leaned down and brushed a soft kiss across Candy's forehead. "We are going to get through this," he assured her with tears swelling in his own eyes. The pair remained in silence staring out the window both wondering where do they go from here.

After a couple of days, Candy was released from the hospital. She tried to assure Zay that she was okay enough to return to LA, but Zay told her that she was going to return to Vegas with him, and he would drive her down that weekend. Zay was actually enjoying the time that he was spending with Candy. It reminded him of the times they spent together when they first met.

Money was a powerful thing because once the pair started making money, Zay stopped looking at Candy as a friend and she became his *business associate.* Candy was truly smart and funny, but Zay stopped paying attention to her in this way a long time ago.

It was Thursday, and Zay still hadn't spoken to Dionni. He tried to contact her periodically since she left him in Detroit. Zay left the hospital a couple hours after Candy woke up, but when he arrived, as he already presumed, Dionni was gone. He tried her cell, office, and home numbers, but each time he reached her voicemail.

The first time, he left her a message saying that he had an emergency and his phone lost signal, which was why it kept going to voicemail. He continued to call her, but Dionni was not paying Zay any attention. He was starting to miss the sound of her voice and the way that her eyes sparkled when she laughed. He knew that he was the one in the wrong.

Once he got back to Vegas, he ordered Candy upstairs to her room and asked her to make a list of everything that she needed. He was going to the store and wanted to make her as comfortable as possible. He waited patiently as she compiled her list and explained to her not to answer the phones just in case Dionni called.

Candy nodded and retreated back upstairs. Zay could have sworn he seen tears start to swell again in Candy's eyes, but when he called her back into the room she had a smile plastered on her face and her eyes were dry. Zay shook it off and asked her was she sure that was it. Candy confirmed her order with Zay and he left.

The first place Zay went was to Dionni's house. He wanted to catch her before she came to the house and caught Candy there. At her house, Zay did not get a response but he was not so sure if she really wasn't there or not. Dionni explained to Zay how when Dale dropped by and started his tantrum at the door she would cover her puppy's mouth and quickly tiptoe up the stairs. Zay would laugh and say that Dale was a fool, but now look at him.

He ran back to his car and jotted down a short note to Dionni stating that he was back in town, and that he wanted to see her. He also told her that there was a change in his plans and that he would be leaving to Los Angeles tomorrow instead of Saturday. He stuck the note into her door and jumped back into his whip.

He knew that Dionni was upset, but he hoped that she would at least give him a call. He knew that if they spoke that night, and came to an understanding, once he returned from LA they could continue where they left off in Detroit, and the make up could begin.

*Was Dionni truly not there, or was she pretending to be gone?*

Zay did not want to be a statistic as well and retreated back to his Aliante neighborhood to the Super

Wal Mart. He grabbed everything off of Candy's list and added two yellow roses to the cart. He knew that roses were her favorite and wanted to cheer her up. She still haven't shared with Zay the entire story of what happened between her and Frank. She pretending that she was okay and was over what was done, but Zay could see that Frank hurt her terribly.

He already had the word out for Frank to be dealt with, but wanted to know *exactly* what happened so that he could make sure that everything that the bastard did to Candy was going to be inflicted on him. He wanted this clown to feel the same way dude did in *Pulp Fiction* when he was raped, but unlike Ving Rhymes, this man was not going to have a chance to get revenge.

Zay was already getting pissed off all over again and had to calm down. Nobody took advantage of anything or anyone that he cared about, and Candy was one of the first on the list of not to be fucked with. Zay shook it off and stopped at TGIF and ordered them some takeout. Before he pulled back up to his house, he looked around to make sure he did not catch a glimpse of Dionni's car. When he seen that the coast was clear, he proceeded into the driveway.

Dionni must not have gotten his note because she still hadn't called. She could not possibly still be holding a grudge and she did not know what really happened. Anything could have happened to him, and she jumped up and left.

Zay had already convinced himself that if Dionni tried to start a shouting match, that bringing up the fact that she *didn't* know what happened was going to be how he reversed the situation back onto her. Smiling, Zay entered the house.

Zay paused; the aroma of fried fish was coming from the kitchen. *What the hell is this girl doing?* Zay thought to himself walking into the kitchen. Upon entrance, Zay had to stop again. Candy was dressed in a short, black, silk night gown that barely covered the thickness of her ass. Her long legs were shining and her hair was pinned up with a clip. She stood in his gourmet kitchen before the stove placing a batch of battered covered fish into the hot frying pan. A platter of golden brown catfish fillets were sitting on the counter, along with some macaroni and cheese and biscuits.

"Candy, what the hell are you doing?" Zay asked her, placing his bags down onto the island. "I picked up some food from Friday's and got everything from the store. You know I wanted you to rest before you went back to LA. Why are you up in here cooking? It smells good and I appreciate it, but at the same time, you are supposed to be in the bed."

Candy turned and gave Zay a genuinely warm and caring smile. "I just wanted to thank you for everything that you have done for me. I know that fried catfish is your favorite meal, and I bet that the *Princess* that you have been dating don't even know her way around the kitchen." She turned her attention back to the food and continued what she was doing.

Zay shrugged his shoulders and took the bags that he brought for her upstairs to her room. He placed the items on her bed, removing the roses from the bag, and came across a picture of him and Dionni lying on the dresser. "What the fu—" Zay said out loud, wondering how that picture ended up in here. It was stuck into his dresser mirror, and he knew that his door was locked. To confirm, he walked down the hallway to his bedroom and tried his door. Just like he thought, the door was locked, so how the hell did she get the picture?

He went downstairs to confront Candy. He found her in the dining room setting up the table for what appeared to be a romantic dinner for two. She brought out his expensive china from the curio, and even cracked open a bottle of Moet.

She turned when she heard him come up behind her and a gigantic smile came across her face when she noticed the roses in his hand. "Are those for me?" she asked and placed the rest of the items into their respected places. Before he could respond, she quickly ran up and planted a kiss firmly onto his parted lips.

Zay was caught off guard and was frozen into his spot. Candy thought the lack of reaction meant that he wanted her to continue, so she did, this time with an open mouth kiss. Automatically, she wrapped her arms up around his neck and entwined her fingers into his hair.

At first, Zay did respond, but when he realized that this was Candy, he attempted to push her away.

"What the fuck are you doing?" Zay exclaimed to Candy. "And what the hell is this doing in your room?" he asked, holding up the picture so that she could see. "How the hell did you get this? My room was locked so how did you get in? You got a key to my shit?" he asked her, really not giving her a chance to respond.

"Zay, you already know that I have a key to the house so why are you acting brand new?" she responded nonchalantly, walking back to the table.

"Candy, you better quit fucking with me." Zay started off as calmly as he could, stepping up behind her. "I had all the locks changed, but I am not talking about the front door, I am making reference to my bedroom. How the hell did you get in there, and why the fuck did you kiss me? You know that we don't get down like that."

Zay was not going to play with Candy today. Since Sasha left, she had been acting totally out of character, but he never made mention to it. He thought it had something to do with her move to California.

Zay thought that was a good idea because that would put some distance between them, and then she could concentrate on herself more. He wanted her to establish herself as a woman by herself, and not in his shadows. He thought that her cool attitude was part of her transition, but right now, he was not too sure.

Candy continued to ignore his questions, now making him a plate, and the silence was just pissing Zay off even more.

"Bitch! You don't hear me talking to you? Do you think I am some kind of punk nigga that you can ignore? You better get to explaining and quick or-or-, you better just get to fucking talking and now, Candice!"

Zay was so upset he was turning red. His chest was heaving and his eyes were starting to fill with hate. He had done everything that he could to look out for her, and yea, majority of the times she deserved it, but right now, she had him fucked up.

"Negro, did you just sit there and call me a bitch?" Candy responded back stepping up to Zay. "You have *NEVER* called me a bitch, but now that you with that funny colored eyed bitch, you think you can disrespect me? Yea, I d*id* go into your room, I removed the key from the ring when you went to the bathroom. I don't understand why you always lock your self away from me! And, *YEA,* I was looking at that picture of you and that *BITCH*! So WHAT!!!" she hollered at Zay.

"I have been selling my pussy for you for *YEARS,* nigga, so I think I have the RIGHT to go anywhere in this house that I damn well please. I am so tired of walking around here on eggshells! I was good enough to walk around this fucking house and every other one that you have had when I was helping you raise your sister like she was my own, but now that she gone, you act like I am a fucking stranger!"

"The only time you have me around is when you got one of your clients that want your *filet mignon*, but other than that you got me baby sitting your flock of young bitches. Do your precious Dionni know about that? Does she know that you are one of the biggest **PIMPS** that Vegas have to offer? A Don Juan Protégé himself?"

"I was just raped, Zay! And I was raped for you! You had me fly to Detroit. You said it was so important to meet your friend, *his pockets are like a river flowing*," she said, mocking Zay. "You set me up, and that fool beat and raped me. Said you owe him! And while I was crying out for you, you were over there fucking **THAT BITCH!**"

Candy was screaming at the top of her lungs so neither of them heard Dionni creep up behind them. Candy was right up in Zay's face appearing as if she was going to hit him. Zay was about to respond, but was interrupted by Dionni.

"I am sorry I interrupted this lover's quarrel."

Zay and Candy both jumped when they heard Dionni's voice. She came out of the hallway shaking, clutching Zay's letter.

"Bab-" Zay started off, attempting to move but was frozen in his spot.

*Oh My God!!! Did she just hear everything? This bitch better not have fucked my shit up! After all I have done for her? How can I explain this to Dionni? Candy half naked and shit, ranting and raving.... I wonder if she heard her say that she was in Detroit and that I'm a pimp?*

So many things were running through Zay's head. He just did not know exactly what to say. He had been trying so hard to prevent Dionni from finding out exactly what ties that he had to Candy, but now all of his attempts have been done in vain.

Before he could finish his word, Dionni interjected.

"So that is why Candy is so important. She is your bottom bitch. That is the right word for you, isn't it?" Dionni said this directing her attention to Candy. "When was the last time he fucked you? I know that's why you sell your self for a man, right? He's your Daddy, right? And when you did, did you at least use a condom? You know what? You don't have to answer that, I don't even fucking want to know. Wow, I have been fucking a pimp. Wow."

Candy didn't respond. Instead, she sat down in a chair at the kitchen table and wept. Dionni must not have felt any sympathy for her, because she just did an about face and began to walk out.

Before she was completely out of sight, she called over her shoulder to Zay, "All my shit that is here, you can go ahead and keep it. Please do not call my phone or come back to my house. I thought you wanted to talk…. Ain't that some shit….That's why you left me at the hotel, to go save your hoe? I guess that is how that go, right, she is your investment, *Mr. Investment Banker.*"

Dionni proceeded out the door. Zay didn't know what to do. The entire scene that just took place was going in slow motion. Do he go after to her or do he just chuck it up to the game? Since he started messing with Dionni, his whole outlook on life was starting to change.

He did not want to deal with the hoes anymore. He did not have to protect Candy anymore. She was on the street along time before Zay met her. Candy was the one who propositioned Zay with the idea of her hoeing for him. She told them that they could come up together.

At first, Zay was uncomfortable with the idea, but after she brought him his first five hundred dollars, all doubts floated out of his mind. The money came so easily and steady that he would have been a fool to let it go. His sister was being taken care of, and all he did was collect the money.

Candy worked solo for the first year, but then went out and recruited a girl here or there. She recruited so many that he had at least two on each coast of the US. Technically, Candy was the *Bottom Bitch,* and she managed those chicks. She really did not have to work anymore unless she choose to. All she had to do was sit back and collect money. He did not know why the hell she was tripping.

At first, Zay thought that she was just dedicated to the game, but after a couple of years, he figured out her prime objective. Candy thought that if she recruited enough chicks then she would not have to work anymore. Zay felt that Candy really believed that they could continue to manage his mini empire together and in the end they would be together.

Zay knew from the beginning that he would never be with Candy. He loved the money that they were making together, but he could n*ever* be with her. Candy was a prostitute. She sold her body and sucked men's dicks for money. He was cool on that.

Zay was not saying that he did not care about her, because in all reality he did. How could you not love someone who brought you all of their money and did everything in their power to keep you happy?

Zay knew he let this shit go on too long. He was making enough money on his own to live comfortably, but he held on to Candy and the others for security. Zay had to make up his mind on which one was more important, his security or Dionni. He knew had to do some soul searching and come up with a plan and quick because the woman that *he* wanted just literally walked out of his life.

# Chapter 10

"I can't believe this shit!" Dionni yelled out the window. She was in her car on her way to her mother's house. Tears were streaming down her face as she sped through the lights not caring if she got pulled over. After calling her mother to let her know she was on her way over, she turned off her cell phone completely. This shit felt like de'ja' vu all over again, only this time with Zay not Dale.

Dionni really did not want to include her mother in her mess, but she knew that Zay would probably be on his way to her house and she really did not want to see him. Zay had met Asha, but he did not know where she lived. After Dale's surprise visit to her mother, Dionni told herself that she would not take another man over there again unless they were married. Dionni was a grown ass woman and did not need her mother as a mediator whenever she and the man in her life were not seeing eye to eye.

Dionni was tired of catching these niggas doing dirt. She knew that she had established feelings for Zay. He made her happy and was always so sweet and courteous, but in the back of her head, she knew that something just wasn't right. She just couldn't put her finger on it.

During her flight back to Vegas the only thing that Dionni could think about was if Candy was in Detroit. Zay took his time catering and pampering Dionni, so to wake up alone really hurt Dionni's feelings. The only time Zay appeared unlike himself was whenever Candy was around. Dionni knew that Candy had been out of sight since Zay changed the locks, but she was not sure if she had been out of his mind.

She has been going back and forth with herself since she touched back down in town. Dionni was so pissed at Zay and tried to convince herself to write him off, but when the messages began to come on her voicemail from him, she could not help but miss him. Over the past couple months, the two of them had begun to spend so much time with each other that Dionni had to admit to herself he had truly become a major factor in her life.

Because of Dionni's forewarning of her arrival, Asha had the garage door already open welcoming her to come in. Dionni pulled in and closed the garage door behind her. Stepping into the house, the scent of her favorite strawberry tea brewing was in the air.

Asha could sense that there was something wrong with her daughter by the tone in her voice when they were on the telephone. She hated when her child was upset and wanted her to calm down.

Dionni found her mother in the kitchen placing sliced mangos, strawberries, and cantaloupe onto a plate. Asha looked into her baby's eyes and could see the pain that was brimming was about to spill over. She stopped what she was doing and gave Dionni a great big hug. Fresh tears streamed down Dionni's cheeks as she placed her head down onto her mother's shoulder.

"Shh, shh, shh," Asha said soothingly into Dionni's while rubbing her back. "What happened, Chile?" It was hurting Asha to see her child cry and hurt in this manner. Even as a child, Dionni was always the strongest out of the four girls. Asha was getting upset watching the tears rush down Dionni's face.

Asha was completely oblivious of what could have possibly transpired that night. She knew that Dionni started dating this new guy, Zay, and had been on cloud nine. Asha liked Zay, but felt that Dionni jumped into the relationship head first.

Asha consoled Dionni a few more moments and lead her into the family room. She had Dionni take a seat in her favorite recliner and fetched the tray of fruit and tea for her daughter. Once they were both settled and Dionni took a couple of sips of tea, Asha then repeated her original question,

"What happened?"

Dionni took some deep breaths and told her mother the entire story. Dionni confessed to her mother how she was confused. She gave her mother step by step details of how her relationship with Zay had progressed over the past several months. She told her how happy Zay made her feel, but there was something always telling her to protect her feelings. Dionni figured that the mental warnings that she was experiencing was just her mind trying to protect her due to all of the pain that Dale left her feeling.

Dionni wanted so badly to be loved and unconditionally. She wanted to be the only woman in a man's life and she was beginning to think that she found that devotion in Zay. She *thought* she came at this relationship with a different approach. She told her mother how she waited before they began to have sex, and how she fore warned him of bits and pieces of her past that hurt in hopes that he paid attention and would not allow history to repeat it self in their situation.

Dionni paused and watched the expression on her mother's face. Asha was listening intensely, waiting for the plot of Dionni's story to thicken.

Dionni fast forward to the trip to Detroit and told her mother how gentle and attentive Zay was to Dionni. She explained to her mother how special he made her feel before she fell asleep and then how sad she was when he never returned to the room or responded to her messages.

Dionni confessed how she drowned herself into her work upon her arrival back in Vegas to prevent herself from communicating with Zay. A part of Dionni was relieved when Zay began calling her, but was pissed off that it took his so long to call. Dionni was curious about what may have happened to Zay, but after all of her years dealing with Dale, really just wanted to see if he was going to lie to her or just come clean.

This was why Dionni was happy when she came home and found the note in the door. She was missing Zay and felt that she gave him enough time to think. Dionni contemplated if she should call Zay or just go over there, and after discussing it with Eva and Tiana, she just went over there. Dionni told her mother how she had a key to his house and just let herself in.

When she walked in, she heard a woman screaming at the top of her lungs. Dionni didn't know who it was and was starting to get pissed off. Dionni crept closer towards the kitchen, where the yelling sounded like it was coming from. She heard the female voice yell at Zay stating that she has been selling her self for him for all of these years and how he is a Don Juan protégé.

"Mom, he's a pimp!" Dionni exclaimed aloud creating a volcano of tears to erupt from her eyes. "I knew something wasn't right with his situation with Candy, but I thought that they were just messing around. I did not know he had her prostituting herself for him. And, Mom, that is not the best part, he got others as well. He has to be sleeping with Candy because she said that she has been doing this for years. No one is going to sell their body for a man with no strings attached! This mess is so crazy!!!"

Dionni continued on with her story reliving everything that she heard and told her mother how she interrupted them and told them both how she felt. By this time, Dionni was yelling at the top of her lungs. She was mad at herself for even letting him into her life like that. She should have kept the relationship completely platonic. If she did, he would not have been able to hurt her feelings as badly.

Dionni was becoming so comfortable with Zay. She thought he was her knight in shining armor, but she now understood what the phrase meant *everything that glitters is not gold.* Dionni stopped and started to stare at the entertainment center. She couldn't be completely upset at Zay though. Dionni hadn't been all the way honest with Zay or herself.

Asha thought that Dionni was finished and she was about to give her daughter some advice, but before she could speak, Dionni continued. "Mom, I can't be mad at Zay though, I was just using him."

Dionni then proceeded to confess to her mother how her feelings for Dale, never completely left her system. Dionni wanted Zay to make all of her memories and feelings for Dale to magically disappear. She wanted to be free of the hold that Dale still had on her. Dionni told her mother how Dale continued to call her and how she felt when she seen him in the pet store. She missed Dale so badly, but thought that if she kept her time occupied, then all thoughts of him would disappear.

A fresh set of tears now trickled down Dionni's face. This time they were tears of confusion. Dionni was remembering the good times that she and Dale have experienced over the years and was starting to question if there was something wrong with her approach.

"Mommy, what's wrong with me? Am I doing something wrong?"

The pair sat in silence as Dionni wept.

Asha finally broke the silence. "Dionni, have you spoken to Dale?"

Dionni looked up at her mother with a puzzled look on her face. *Was she not listening to her? I thought I just said I seen Dale in the pet store?*

Reading Dionni's thoughts, Asha spoke again. "I am not saying spoken to him in passing, I mean spoken to him and tell him how you felt? Have you given him or yourself any closure? I think that you jumped into that situation with Zay. You need to get up tomorrow and get yourself tested. You know that condoms are not one hundred percent protection so you can still catch something. By the way, you *have* been using protection right?"

Dionni nodded but didn't even think about this shit from that perspective. One thing Dionni believed in was safe sex, especially after all the times that she has been to the clinic to ensure she was healthy after finding out about another one of Dale's indiscretions. This time she thought shit was different. She was slipping.

"Okay, once you get that taken care of, I think that you should reach out to Dale and sit down and talk. You can not start another chapter with some else if the original book was never completed. I am not saying that Dale was not wrong because he was, but you never resolved anything. Are you two friends, enemies, or what? Now baby girl, you got two chapters to close instead of just one. I feel for you."

Dionni glanced at her mother shaking her head and began to giggle. She always have the right answer even if it is not what you want to hear.

"Mommy, I love you." Dionni wiped the tears away from her eyes and walked over to her mother kissing her on the forehead. "I will be okay; I just needed that constructive intervention. I don't think I am going to go home though, I need some time by myself to figure out how these chapters are going to end."

"Well, I am glad that I could have been some assistance to you, I guess," Asha told Dionni giving her a hug.

Dionni finished her fruit and tea, and spoke to her mother for a few more minutes.

Asha yawned, confessing how tired she was all of a sudden. It was two in the morning, and she had to get up early. Asha brought Dionni a quilt to cover herself with and left her alone to think about what she was going to do next.

Dionni unfolded the blanket and made herself comfortable on the couch. She closed her eyes trying to not to think about her life. Dionni wanted to have a peaceful, dreamless sleep. She prayed to God to give her a clear mind and heart that would allow her to make rational decisions in the area of her life from this day forth. She turned over and attempted to fall asleep.

Stretching her arms out, Dionni reached out for Dior, but instead her arm fell down and was greeted by the coolness of the tiled floor. Sitting up, Dionni had to remember exactly where she was at.

Dionni's prayers were answered and she fell asleep in solitude. She did not dream about anything which allowed her to rest. Looking around the room scenes from the night before rushed into her head.

Shaking off any negative thoughts, Dionni got up and fixed her mother's house. Asha was gone to work already and did not want her to come home to the mess from the night before. Dionni freshened herself up and hurried home. Dior was locked up from the night before and she knew she had to hurry before the puppy had an accident.

Dionni was halfway home before she remembered she needed to make an appointment for a quick check up. Dionni confirmed an appointment with her gynecologist for that afternoon and decided that she was going to call Dale. Her mother was right, and she needed to get all of her ducks in order with everyone before she went insane!

Later that day, Dionni was leaving her doctor's office relieved that all of her test came out negative. She said a small prayer to God thanking him for continuing to look after her and drove out of the parking lot. She was going to go to the office, but was not ready to see anyone yet.

Her mother was the only person that knew about what happened with Zay the night before and she did not want to talk about it. That morning when she powered on her cell phone, she noticed that Zay left her a couple of messages, but she deleted them all before even listening to them.

He was the last person that she wanted to talk

too. The entire time that she was on the examination table Dionni prayed to God that if he allowed these test to come out negative, that she would go to church **EVERY** Sunday and would even go to bible study on Wednesday nights.

After the nurse gave her the clean bill of health, Dionni left and decided that it was time to give Dale a call. Dionni agreed completely with what Asha said. She knew that in the beginning she was using Zay as a scapegoat to get over Dale. She tried to keep herself occupied so that she wouldn't have a chance to let Dale back in, but now looking back *was that really a good idea?*

If someone would have told her this time last year that a person could care about two people at the same time, Dionni would have begged a differ. She thought that a person could only care about one person at a time, but looking at this mess that she has created with Dale and Zay, Dionni wasn't too sure.

Jumping on the freeway, Dionni's head was beginning to hurt. She did not know what to say to Dale or even how to start the conversation. *What am I going to say to say to him, 'Hey Dale how are you doing?'* Dionni did not know how he was going to react to her phone call. She blew off all of his attempts of communication, so why should he give her a chance to speak now?

Dionni decided to call on her friends for their advice on what exactly should she do. She was not sure on how they were going to react to her question, but at the present moment she really didn't care if they thought that she was crazy. Dionni knew that she was going to have to tell them what happened with Zay, but right now the only thing she was going to talk about was Dale

Dionni called Tiana and Eva on three-way. She gave them a quick break down on why she wanted to call Dale; conveniently leaving out the part about Candy and Zay. She explained to them that if she really wanted to have a successful relationship with Zay or anyone else, then she knew that she had have this part of her life closed.

The pair listened to their friend completely. They were both confused. Dionni and Zay seemed to be so happy, but maybe something happened. They both knew that when she was ready she would tell them where this revelation came from, but had to help her with her question at hand.

"Be careful," Tiana said to her after Dionni

explained her situation.

The phone went completely silent for a moment or two.

"What do you think Eva," Dionni asked her other friend who was just listening quietly to everything Dionni had to say.

"Girl, I don't know exactly what to say on that subject. I don't know where this is coming from, but see where the conversation takes you. I like Zay, but I feel I have been knowing Dale for a long time. I know that Dale do love you, even if he is fucked up. All I got to say is talk to him and see what happens."

Tiana sighed in disgust interrupting her friend's speech. "That is the worst bullshit that I have heard you say in a long time, and girl you know you can say some shit. You know that Dale is a bullshit artist, and Dionni falls short for everything that the fool has to say. All the tricking off that he was doing, and you think that she should talk to him? All I got to say is just be careful. You can't help who you love, but don't be stupid either."

The phone went silent again. Dionni did not expect the conversation to go like this. They really did not say too much and Dionni was disappointed. She really needed their help. Thanking them both, Dionni excused her self and ended the conversation. Hopping on the freeway, Dionni decided to head home and contact Dale later on that night.

# *Chapter 11*

"Hey, Dale, you asleep?" Dionni whispered into the telephone.

Dale was awakened by the singing of his cell phone. "Me and My Girlfriend" was the ring tone that he heard, but Dale thought that he was still dreaming by the sound. He hadn't heard that ring tone in months. The first time the phone started to ring, Dale turned over in his bed as he saw Dionni's pretty face behind his eye lids.

The second time he heard his phone ring, Dale laid on his back and reached for his phone on the night table.

"Damn, it really is Dionni," he said, sitting up.

Dale took a moment before he responded. He wanted to make sure he did not appear too anxious while speaking to her.

"Yea, ma, you cool. What's up?" Dale's heart skipped a beat waiting to hear Dionni's voice again.

"Um, I was wondering if I could," Dionni stammered, taking a couple of deep breaths. When Dionni heard Dale's voice, a slight flutter ran through the pit of her stomach. Dionni had to agree with her mother that this conversation was long overdue and she hoped that in the end the two of them would experience closure.

"What's wrong, D?" Dale asked. "Why are you stuttering?" Dale was really confused. Dionni was always ready for every situation, so to hear her choked up was mind blowing to him. "What were you wondering?"

Dionni paused and took another deep breath. Slowly she started to speak again. "Dale, I was wondering if you could come over so we could talk." There, she said it. Dionni did not understand why it was so hard for her to get her words together. She rehearsed this conversation to herself in the mirror for the past couple of hours, but was experiencing a brief lost for words.

She hoped Dale would not ask too many questions and would just come by. Dionni hoped that Dale would just be happy to hear her request. When she first came up with this plan, she was going to go to Dale's house, but decided against it.

Antwan and the crew could have been over, and Dionni wasn't ready to face any of his friends or family yet. At least at her house it was only Dior there to judge, and Dionni knew that her puppy was always on her side.

Dale paused and didn't say a thing.

He had so many different things going on in his head. He reached down and started to rub the second head that he used to formulate decisions. His tool grew just by the sound of her voice. He missed Dionni so much.

"Yeah, I can come over if you want me to. Are you sure you want me to? You know it is kind of late."

"Dale, can you please just come?"

Dale sensed the urgency in Dionni's voice and decided that it would be best if he got his ass over there and quickly.

Thirty minutes later, Dale was parked in front of Dionni's house gripping the steering wheel with moist hands.

*This shit is crazy. Why do I feel like a kid about to get punished by his momma? I wonder what is really going on. Maybe I should just go home.*

Answering his question for him, Dionni opened the front door. She wore a Cowboy's jersey and a pair of thick wool socks.

Seeing her in his jersey made a slight smile appear at the corner of his lips, but quickly disappeared when Dionni turned and walked away, not smiling back.

There was much tension as Dale entered the house. Dionni had to catch her breath real quick while he walked past her and the scent of his cologne lingered behind.

*He hasn't lost his sex appeal,* Dionni thought while biting her bottom lip leading him into the kitchen.

He wore a white tee, denim jeans, white forces, and a platinum cross hung from his neck. He looked around, wondering if this would be the last time he was going to be invited back. He walked over to the couch in the den and sat down.

Dionni was in the kitchen nervous as hell. She didn't know what to say or remember how to tell him everything that she had practiced. It was almost three in the morning, and typically this would have been perfect booty call hours for the duo, but Dionni didn't want to go that route.

"Would you like something to drink?" Dionni asked, peering into the open refrigerator. "I have red stripe, water, iced tea, and --" Dionni paused with a smile on her face, looking away. "Peach juice."

"Peach juice."

This comment was amusing to Dale as well. A

Kool-Aid smile appeared on his face as he watched her pour the drink. This was Dale's favorite beverage, and it surprised him that she would still have some in her ice box. His smile soon turned into a frown as he wondered if Dionni was sharing their drink with someone else.

Watching Dale's mood change from happy to distraught, Dionni quickly understood.

"I'm the only one who drinks it. I guess it's a reminder of you."

An awkward silence fell over the room. Neither one of them knew what to say. Dale still didn't know the reason Dionni requested him to come over, so he used his curiosity to break the silence.

"So, what's up?"

Dionni stared at Dale for a moment and finally walked over to give him his drink. She wandered into the living room and settled herself on the couch sitting Indian style. Dale sat across from her.

Uncomfortable, Dionni gripped a throw pillow and took a few deep breaths.

Clearing her throat, she finally began.

"Well, I know that this situation is weird as hell, but I finally gained the confidence to speak to you. I decided to do it face to face before my nerves got the best of me again."

Dale sat there quietly giving Dionni his undivided attention.

"I believe that we ended this relationship on a sour note, and through everything, why can we not be friends. After all this time, I feel as if we rushed into having sex and maybe we should have worked harder on our friendship in the beginning. We were together for way too long to just disappear out of each other's life completely."

Dionni paused to see how Dale was responding to her speech. He just sat their staring at her appearing as if he really understood where she was coming from.

Dionni continued.

"You have hurt me so badly. I don't think that I could ever explain to you how bad. This shit is really fucking with me. I did everything as a woman that I thought was good, but you still dogged me on so many different occasions."

Dionni began to choke up.

"I just want to know one thing. Why did you do all of that shit to me? What was I doing wrong? Why didn't I make you happy? Why couldn't I have been enough for you?"

Questions were flying out of Dionni's mouth at the same rate the tears were streaming down her face. She proceeding in telling him how all of his acts of infidelity made her feel less of a woman. Dionni was crying and heaving, smothering her face into her pillow.

Dale came over and pulled Dionni into his arms.

"I am so sorry, ma, really I am. Please stop crying."

He hated to see Dionni cry. After all this time apart, Dionni's tears still had an effect on him. He soothed her, softly wiping the tears away from her eyes. When she appeared to have slightly calmed down, he softly kissed her on the forehead.

"Go get dressed," he said. "Let's go get a drink. You really need one."

Dionni began to chuckle. She knew that she looked a hot mess, and the emotional break down that she just experienced did not make it any better. Slowly, she agreed and went upstairs to change her clothes.

Dale admired Dionni's natural beauty as she came down the stairs wearing a white sundress and white strappy sandals. Her hair was brushed over her shoulder and she wore no makeup.

"You ready?" Dale asked her with a smile on his

face.

"Yes, sir, I am," she said and followed him out the door.

"You bought a new car," she asked as they climbed into an Audi coupe.

"Yeah, I am trying to make some life changes, so I started with the car. Do you like it?"

Dionni nodded as she got settled into the car.

Fifteen minutes later, the pair was seated in a booth in the back of the lounge that they used to frequent when they first met.

In the beginning their conversation was intense, but as the night progressed and several rounds of drinks later; they found themselves snuggled up to each other laughing reminiscing on the good times.

When a yawn released from Dionni's lips, Dale suggested that they should go.

Glancing down at her watch, Dionni realized what time it was and confirmed Dale's suggestion of calling it a night. "It's almost five and I have to meet a client at eight. I just landed this deal, and I can't afford to be fucking up."

Disappointed that she agreed, Dale respected her wishes and took her back home. During the drive, Dale and Dionni sat in complete silence. Dale was happy that even after all of their time apart their conversation never skipped a beat. Seeing Dionni laugh really confirmed to Dale that he was going to do whatever it took to get their relationship back on track. Dale wanted Dionni to go home with him, and Dionni had one last question to him.

At the lounge, Dale answered all of Dionni's questions but one. He admitted to everything that Dionni already knew, but could not prove it. Dale would stick to his story at all times whenever Dionni would question him during their relationship, but now he was singing a different tune.

Dale pulled up to Dionni's house. Dale looked at Dionni and could see that something was bothering her, and he wanted to know what was on Dionni's mind. He watched her closely as he answered all of her questions about different women and compromising situations. She didn't react, and quiet frankly, a look of relief actually came across her face. So now her sudden mood changes were making Dale nervous.

"What's wrong, babe?" he asked.

"Why didn't I make you happy?"

Dionni interrupted Dale's thoughts. He turned and looked out the window. After all their time apart,

Dale was ready for this question. After several more seconds, Dale finally responded.

"You did make me happy," Dale said, turning and looking her dead in the eyes. "I just didn't know how to make you happy. I didn't know how to love you, Dionni. If you would give me a chance to earn your trust back, I will do everything in my power to make you happy and to make up for lost time."

Dionni didn't respond. She wasn't sure how to feel about the response that he gave. Dale and Dionni searched each other's eyes, trying to read each other's thoughts.

"Dale, I really got to go."

Dionni got out of the car. Dale got out as well, and walked her to the door.

"Well I really enjoyed myself," he told her while looking intensively into her eyes. Running his fingers through her hair, he leaned in and brushed a quick kiss against her lips.

He sent a sensation through her body that only Dale could make happen. Dale leaned in again and kissed Dionni again. He kissed the bottom lip first slowly and gently, and then repeated the same actions to the top. His hands slid down past her hair and softly down her back. A slight moan escaped her lips and she wrapped her hands around his neck, tenderly massaging his head. He parted her lips with his tongue and kissed her with a little more force, cupping her ass and pulling her closer.

Their embrace lasted for several minutes till Dionni had to break free. She knew that if it lasted any longer, this man would be fucking her in the living room. She was dripping wet between her legs and by the size of the growing knot that she felt, Dionni knew that he could feed that hunger that she had been having.

She ran her fingers down his chest and promised him that she would see him after she got off work.

Once in the house, Dionni exhaled. All of her questions that were haunting her about Dale had finally subsided. All of the feelings that she tried to tuck away for him resurfaced, which scared her. She promised herself that she was not going to rush back into anything with Dale. Dionni did not want her heart to be broken again. She did not know why she let Dale kiss her. She enjoyed it, but that really was not her intentions for their meeting that night.

Dionni wanted to see where Dale's head was at. She knew that if she gave the word, she would be back spending every free chance she got with Dale. Dionni loved the way he made her feel. When they were together, he made her feel special and complete. Dionni sighed again and went up the stairs.

Thinking back on her life from the time that she met Dale to now, Dionni could not understand where their relationship went wrong. He did answer her questions and apologized, but the hurt was still there. She was good to that man and held resentment in her heart for all of the time that she dedicated herself to him. It still blew her mind that he would venture out to these other bitches when he had her at home.

Dionni knew that they had a long road to recovery if they were going to mend their broken relationship, but she had to admit that they were on the right path.

While undressing, Dionni's cell phone began to ring.

"Hello."

"Thank you for giving me a chance to explain myself," Dale's sexy voice swooned across the line.

A smile crept across her face as she replied, "You are welcome. Thank you for being honest with me. As long as stay honest, I don't see why our friendship can't be amended."

Dionni climbed into the bed and stayed on the phone with Dale until he arrived home. They chatted the entire time about Eva and how he missed her just as much as he missed Dionni. When Dionni heard the chirp of Dale's alarm, she knew he was at home.

"I'll talk to you in the morning, I promise," Dionni assured Dale. "I really need to get some sleep."

Reluctantly, Dale agreed and let Dionni go. He was happy that he was finally on his road to redemption and went into the house.


Waiting till the lights went off in Dionni's room, Zay finally turned on his car and drove off.

"Damn, she ain't waste no time," he said. "Back fucking with that nigga already." Zay wanted to follow Dale and whoop his ass, but he knew that he was not the one in the wrong.

As much shit as she talked about dude, she sure did oblige as he kissed her and felt on her booty. Zay was so upset, but knew that it was his fault that she even called Dale over.

Dionni called him earlier that day and left a quick message on his office phone stating that she was going to get tested. He understood where she was coming from after finding out in such a way that Candy was a prostitute. He knew that if he told her that he has never had sex with Candy, she would not believe him, but hell, it was the truth.

He had been camped out in front of Dionni's neighbor's house since about midnight in the new Mercedes coupe that he purchased for Dionni before the Detroit incident. He wanted to talk to her and still hand her the keys of her new whip, but was trying to work up the nerve. Every time he called her, she sent him to voicemail. He knew that she was still awake because the lights were still on in her house and he would occasionally see her walk past the kitchen window.

He finally got the nerve to get out and knock on the door when an Audi pulled up. Zay never seen Dale up close, but he knew that it was him as soon as he saw Dale's face. Zay sat in the car gripping the steering wheel. Zay decided to wait and watch what was going to happen.

Zay sat outside and watched the house until he saw the pair leave and hop into Dale's ride. Zay waited until they were at the corner before he started his car and proceeded to follow them. He followed them until they reached the Peppermill and they went inside.

Still wanting to see what was going to happen, he waited for them to come outside. Zay dozed off several times waiting for them. By the time that they walked out, the sun was starting to rise.

Zay was past pissed off. If he would have just told Dionni the truth in the beginning about Candy, they would not have been in this situation. How the hell was he going to fix this shit?

Continuing to follow them, Zay was relieved when Dionni went into the house alone. He was upset about the kiss, but he decided to chop that to the game. He would let that nigga Dale have that one, but in the end, he would have his girl back.

This time alone that Dale had to experience only allowed him to start thinking for himself. He thought about why he was in the predicament he was in. He knew that his indiscretions with the opposite sex and his living situation were two of the main conflicts of interest that he had and he was determined to correct it.

# *Chapter 12*

All of the rumors that Tiana heard about Dionni and Dale were correct. They had been spending more time together, which in turn applied a strain to their relationship. At work, Dionni spoke to Eva and they cracked jokes and laughed, but whenever Tiana asked Dionni about Dale her response was, "We're cool." David and Eva told her that Dionni was happy, and no doubt, Tiana wanted the best for her friend.

She just was uncomfortable on the subject of Dale. There was something that she knew about Dale that she had kept a secret for a long time. Tiana wanted to talk to Dionni, but did not know how to approach her.

A couple of years back, Tiana used to date Antwan. Antwan wasn't living with Dale yet and had an apartment in North town. Antwan was at work and locked himself out of his car. Peering into the window, he could see the keys sitting on the passenger seat.

It was midnight and Antwan was tired and did not want to wait around for pop a lock to come. He just needed to get into his spot and Dale had his spare keys. Antwan called Dale a couple of times. After the fifth time with no response, he called Tiana. Fifteen minutes later she picked Antwan up and was going to take him back to her house till the morning.

Antwan reminded her of the trip that Dionni was taking Dale on for his birthday and had to catch him before they left. Dionni had found out that she was pregnant and was going to surprise Dale with a trip to Cancun.

Everyone knew about the surprise trip, but only Tiana knew about the baby. Reluctant, Tiana drove Antwan to Dale's house. She was so tired and wanted to get back into bed, but knew that they might miss Dale in the morning and she was not going to play chauffer to Antwan all weekend.

Antwan rang the doorbell a couple of times, but after no response figured that Dale must have been at Dionni's house. He had the pass code to the garage keypad in his cell phone, but had to pee really badly. He went into the backyard to relieve himself and gave Tiana the key pad code.

Tiana played with the code in the dark with the only light coming from the cell phone. After the third try, Tiana got the garage to open and inside was Dale's BMW. Tiana called for Antwan, but he asked her to just go and get the keys off of the key rack in the game room.

After all the times that Tiana had been to Dale's house, she knew her way around and told Antwan that she would be right back.

The house was quiet and dark. As Tiana got to the stairs leading down to the game room, she could hear the sound of music. Tiana called Dale's name a couple of times, but didn't get any response. She continued down the stairs, but things were just not adding up to Tiana. It sounded as if someone was in the house because she could hear laughter, which made the hair stand on her arms.

Tiana called Dale's name again, but still no response. Tiana tried to shake it off and told herself that it must be the television on. She continued down the stairs but had to stop once she reached the second to the last step. Tiana couldn't believe what was going on before her eyes.

Dale was at home, but not alone. He must have been celebrating his birthday early. Dale was laying flat on his back and was getting the ride of his life while one girl sat on his lap and the other one had her ass seated directly on Dale's face. The women were kissing each other, so she never got a chance to see either one of their faces. There was so much moaning and groaning going on, no wonder they did not hear her call his name. Tiana couldn't breathe and almost fainted, but held onto the staircase for support.

She backed out of the room and ran right into Antwan. She did not know how long he had been standing behind her, but at least he saw the same thing she did. Antwan told her to go back upstairs, that he was going to take care of this.

Tiana slowly went up the stairs and back outside. Part of her wanted to know who these chicks were, but she knew that if she came face to face with them she would want to fight. Ending up in jail would not benefit anyone, so she had to think rationally and wait for Antwan to get back into the car.

She got back into her car and couldn't think. So many things were going on in her mind. *How the hell was she going to tell Dionni this bullshit? Was Dionni even going to believe her? Man, why did she have to see this shit? What the hell was taking Antwan so long?*

Tears were streaming down her face and Tiana could barely see. She was so pissed because Dionni was just like a sister to her. Dionni only confided in Tiana about the pregnancy and made her promise not to tell anyone, not even Eva.

When Tiana told Antwan about the trip, she conveniently left out the part about the baby. She was so excited when Dionni told her that she was pregnant and how she went to such great lengths to ensure that this trip would be perfect. Dionni did not deserve this shit.

After what seemed like an eternity, Antwan finally got back into the car. He didn't look at Tiana, he just ordered her to pull off. They were almost at Antwan's apartment before he finally asked her what she was going to do.

"What do you mean, what am I going to do?" Tiana said, snapping her neck in his direction. "I am going to tell my friend that I saw her man fucking two bitches! That is what I am going to do!" This conversation led to a heated argument between the two. Antwan felt that it was not their place to get into their business, but Tiana begged a differ.

Their argument was interrupted by the ringing of Tiana's cell phone.

"Hello!" Tiana yelled into the receiver.

"T, where are you?" Dionni said barely over a whisper.

*Did this fool call her himself?* Tiana thought before responding to her friend.

Clearing her throat, Tiana finally answered. "I am taking Antwan home, why what's up? What's wrong, baby girl?"

"Can you come get me? I think I am losing my baby." Dionni moaned in between cries. She was lying on the floor of her bathroom with a towel shoved between her legs. She had her head buried into her arms trying to regain composure.

Tiana screamed, damn near hitting the car ahead of her. The only person that was family to her was losing her baby while the daddy was getting sucked and fucked by two nasty heifers.

"Girl, I am on my way!" The issue of Dale and his hoes had to be put on the backburner right now because Dionni really needed her. "Calm down, baby girl. You not are losing the baby. Everything is going to be okay. Do you hear me?"

Tiana was crying like a baby, trying to soothe her friend. Antwan just sat in the passenger seat, silent and feeling like shit. If he would have never locked his keys in the car, they would have never gone over to Dale's house, and everything would have been cool.

Tiana ordered Antwan to call the paramedics, and she stayed on the phone with Dionni until they arrived. The EMT took the phone from Dionni and informed her that they would be taking her to Valley Hospital. Once Tiana hung up the phone, she filled Antwan in with the fact that Dionni had not spoken to Dale. The incident that they walked in on was not the cause of Dionni's situation.

They ran to the emergency room where they found Dionni hugging a pillow. She was sobbing silently. Tiana was wondering where was Dale. Antwan finally got him to answer the phone and broke the bad news to him. He said that he was on his way, but that was over fifteen minutes ago. He lived fairly close to the hospital, so Tiana was not taking any excuses.

Before she could ask her question aloud, Dale rushed in with roses in his hand. Moments later, Eva came in with Ms. Asha. Everyone stood around Dionni before the nurse shooed away everyone but Asha, Dale, and Tiana. Everyone was on edge, especially Dale since he did not understand why they were there.

Once the four of them were alone, Dionni finally stated softly, "The baby is gone." Everyone was silent except Dale because he was the last to know about Dionni's secret pregnancy.

"Baby?" Dale said his voice almost a falsetto.

"Yeah," Tiana chimed in. "A baby. She was trying to surprise you and tell you for your birthday in Cancun."

Tears sprang to Dale's eyes as he watched Dionni roll over in the bed and sob into the pillow. He was speechless.

"Baby, I'm sorry, I- I- I didn't know. Damn."

"I tried to call you when the blood started. You would not answer. I needed you."

Dionni wept harder. Asha reached into the bed hugging her child and soothing her with soft words of encouragement. A pregnant silence lingered over the room. Eva stood back, leaning against the wall with tears streaming down her face. Dale stood in his spot, frozen and blame ridden.

His eyes kept wandering from Dionni to Tiana. Tiana glared at him with daggers. Her eyes explained to him that the only reason why she did not say anything was because of the situation at hand.

Tiana was so hurt for her friend, but knew that this was not the time or the place to tell her what she witnessed. She knew that eventually Dionni would leave his trifling ass. The day that Dionni discovered Ashley,

Tiana was relieved that her friend finally caught Dale red handed. Then, when Zay stepped onto the scene, Tiana just knew that Dale really had a run for his money.

But just like that, he was gone. Dionni had not mentioned him at all, and Tiana was wondering what was up with that. They were extremely happy, and poof, he was gone. Tiana wanted to overstep her boundaries and try to contact Zay herself, but she knew that would be out of line.

She had to come at this with a different approach. Dionni was completely tight lipped when it came onto the subject of both of these men, and Tiana wanted to know what Zay did to her friend.

He hadn't tried to come by the office or even call. She knew that he had called Dionni on her cell because she had been there on a couple of occasions when he had called and Dionni would tell him that she was with a client and had to call him back.

Tiana would ask Dionni what's going on, and her only response would be all that glitters is not golden, and would walk off. She knew that whatever Zay had done must have been fucked up, but damn, what did he do? Tiana promised herself that she was going to find out exactly what happened, and she was going to reveal

Dale's secret to Dionni.

Dionni walked into the kitchen and placed her shopping bags down on the island.

*Damn, I'm tired. Maybe I should take a nap before Dale picks me up.* Dionni kicked off her cross trainers and pressed play on the messages on the answering machine.

Since the night that they came to an understanding, Dionni and Dale had spent an abundance of time with each other. They had gone to the movies and dinner almost every night, and Dionni was really enjoying his company.

When Dionni and Dale were not together, they were both texting and instant messaging each other, or they were chatting on the phone until the wee hours in the morning. They were enjoying each other's company sex free, and Dionni felt that the transition that they endured only made them closer.

Listening to the messages, Dionni became upset. Someone was playing on her phone breathing into receiver. There were three messages on the machine, all from an unknown number. She had been getting hanged up calls on both of her phones, and whenever she would let them go to the machine, the person would just sit there and breathe into the line.

She suspected it was Zay at first, but the more consistent the calls became, the more that Dionni knew that it had to be a female. Only a scorned woman would devote so much time into getting on another woman's nerves.

"If this keeps up, I am going to have to call Zay and ask him to tell Candy to please stop calling me," Dionni said while freeing Dior from her kennel and letting her go outside into the backyard. Zay had been getting on her nerves calling her at all hours of the night accusing her of fucking Dale. Dionni felt that she had owed the brother NO explanation at all. It did not matter if she was fucking Dale or not. He was fucking his whore.

Every time he would call her fussing, Dionni would excuse herself off of the phone. Zay would then wait a few moments and call her back apologizing for his outburst. When he saw that his kind words were not getting him anywhere, he would then go back to accusing her of being with Dale.

Zay's tyrants were getting on her nerves. He was tripping because he messed up. Ain't men a trip! Trying to be mad because he fucked up.

It was bad enough to have Zay call so many times throughout the day and night, but now she was receiving prank calls. This shit was getting ridiculous, but Dionni wasn't going to let it put a damper on her plans for the evening. She was going to handle this problem in the morning. She let Dior back in and went upstairs to go take a nap.

# *Chapter 13*

Candy had so many questions that kept running through her head. When Dionni stormed out, Zay left as well. The only thing Candy could make out through her own tears was the order that Zay gave for Candy to be out of his house before he came back. She did not know where Zay went. She heard him leave the room and soon after she heard the garage door open.

Not knowing what to do next, Candy began to pace the floor. It had been three weeks since her fight with Zay and she was going ballistic. Finally, Zay decided to contact her, but by a letter. Candy had to take a seat after she began reading it:

*Candy,*

*What's up, how are you doing? Well as for me, I guess you can say that I am alright considering the obvious. I am sorry that it has taken so long for me to contact you. No special reason that it took so longer other than trying to get my thoughts together be fore I just drafted a letter.*

*First off, I would like to say that you have disappointed me. I know that you are a grown woman, and as well as a human being so you are allowed to make mistakes, but through all of the shit that we have been through, I truly believed that I had a genuine friend in you. This is almost impossible to come by now a days.*

*The first couple of days after you left, I was lost, and really couldn't believe that you were the cause of so much confusion in my life. I would like you to know that your services are no longer needed. I do not feel as if I would be able to trust you again after that performance that you put on. Please do not attempt to contact me any further. If you do not understand this letter, then feel free to contact me via email.*

*It would be in your best interest if you stayed away from me and my family. There is no love loss, you still hold a special place in considering all of the history that we have shared. You were there for Sasha and I thank you. All good things come to an end eventually, but I didn't know our relationship was going to end like this.*

*I am sorry to be so formal, but I think in this situation, it has to be. I promise you, Candy, that if you do not adhere to this letter, I will have legal actions placed against you. I will have you evicted from your home, and everything that I allowed you to utilize because of our business relationship will be repossessed.*

*You signed that disclaimer when Sasha graduated agreeing to these terms, and I promise you, I will use that documentation in court.*

*It was fun while it lasted.*

*Zay*

Candy did not think that Zay would take it this far. She tried to call him, but all of his numbers were disconnected. She even tried to contact Sasha to see how serious Zay was, and her numbers were disconnected as well.

Candy could not believe that her plan backfired in her face like this. She worked on this plot for a while to get rid of Dionni. She thought she had a fool proof plan, but instead of Dionni out of the picture, Zay wanted her gone.

*This is not how this was supposed to end. How did that BITCH get in?* her mind wondered. *Why the hell was I so stupid and did not put that picture back? Thank God he did not check to see if the key to his door was still on the ring. If he found out I bought copies of all the keys to the locks he had changed, he would kill me and Juan. What did she mean, he asked her to come by? She should have been walking into the house seeing some powerful lovemaking transpire.*

Soon after Dionni came into the picture, Zay called Candy and asked her not to come to Vegas for a while. He said that it was important for him to take things to another level with Dionni. Like always, she told him that she understood, and hung up the phone. After all the years that she dealt with Zay, Candy knew him like the back of her hand. She knew the next step was going to be the changing of the locks.

She jumped on a red eye and paid Juan, Zay's locksmith, a visit. She showed up at his office and compensated him very well, financially and physically. After about forty-five minutes, Candy was on her way out with keys to everything Zay owned in tow.

Next she stopped by Zay's house. Looking at the clock on the dashboard of the rental, she realized that it was 9:30 in the morning. Candy knew Zay should be at the office but wanted to make sure.

She gave him a quick call on his cell phone. When he answered, Candy informed him that she was just checking in.

"I'm in a meeting," he said. "I'll call you later."

With this confirmation, Candy smiled and let herself into the house. She walked from room to room, checking out all of the locks. Once everyone had been tested, Candy went into Zay's office and copied all of the pages of his calendar for the next year. Hopefully her plan would not take that long to work and Dionni would be gone sooner, and not later. Candy then went from room to room making sure that everything was back as Zay left it, and like a thief in the night, was on a flight back to Cali.

During the months that followed, Candy was on her best behavior. Everything that Zay asked of her, she obliged. She did not complain about anything. Candy's ultimate goal was to gain Zay's complete trust.

She listened as he spoke about Dionni, and even offered him advice on things he should do for her. She wished him the best in his relationship and told him that she hoped that everything worked out for him.

Since Candy had her own copy of Zay's schedule, she made sure that she was available whenever he had an out of state meeting or event. She wanted to make sure that she was ready and waiting for anything. She made sure that all of the other girls were booked up during those times, and that she was the only one available.

Finally, when Zay summoned her to Detroit, Candy knew she had to put on a stellar performance for her plan to work. When she touched down, Zay gave her instructions on who she was meeting and what she was supposed to do.

Taking her time to get dressed, Candy wanted to make sure she was simply irresistible to her date. When she was finished, she smiled at the appearance that smiled back at her in the full length mirror of the hotel bathroom. She wore a short, white, body hugging dress from the House of Deréon that was completely booty-luscious.

The dress stopped midway down her thigh, and she was completely naked underneath. She contrasted the white with a pair of purple stilettos and a purple Dooney and Burke clutch. She wore no jewelry and a sheer amount of gloss coated her lips. Candy knew Frank would not be able to keep his eyes off of her, and that was all part of the plan.

Once at the restaurant, Candy put on an Academy Award winning performance. She was good at what she did and wasted no time touching, caressing, and whispering all the things that she wanted Frank to do her. She sealed the deal by taking Frank's left hand and rubbing it seductively up her thigh. Once she reached the desired destination, Candy guided Frank's trembling fingers into her warm spot. Not even getting a chance to get through with the appetizers, Frank ordered for the check and the couple left the restaurant, heading back to Frank's hotel room.

Once inside the room, Candy changed face. She informed Frank that she could not go through with things. She told him that she was sorry, but she had to leave. She constantly was tugging at the hem of her dress, blowing Frank's mind away.

Frank could not believe that this was the same woman that couldn't keep her hands off of him less than thirty minutes ago. He also could not believe that this was the same woman that he paid ten thousand dollars for her weekend services. Now, she was acting like a confused school girl.

Getting up to leave, Candy knew that this was really going to piss him off. Her plans worked; as she attempted to unlock the door, Frank dragged her back. Everything else went in a blur for Candy after that. Frank beat and raped her repeatedly for hours. Once he was finished, he forced Candy into the shower and ordered her to get dressed. Making sure she left with everything that she came with, Frank walked her to the elevator and told her to get in.

Candy did not even remember getting to the hospital. Everything seemed surreal to her. Reality sunk back in when the nurse informed her that Mr. Gray was in the waiting room. When she saw that Zay left Dionni and came to her rescue, Candy was elated! When he suggested she fly back to Vegas with him, she was convinced that she could finalize her mission. But she had to be sloppy and leave the picture in her room.

Pouring a shot of Bacardi, Candy thought about what was going to be her next move.

*Should I just leave Zay alone? I have invested so many years into this shit. Hmm.*

Candy finished her drink and began to make a few phone calls. If this shit was truly going to be over, Candy was determined that it was going to be completely on her own terms.

"Okay, baby. I am on my way."

Dionni hung up the phone and sat up in the bed. She was not surprised at the time when she glanced over at the clock. She had a late night flight back into town from Dallas, and she was exhausted. She was in Houston for the past week, coordinating a wedding for a close friend of her mother. Being the perfectionist that Dionni was, she could not leave until she knew that everything was perfect and everyone was completely satisfied.

The sound of the phone ringing interrupted Dionni's precious sleep. Angrily, Dionni answered but when she realized that it was Dale, the anger went away. Instead, Dionni was filled with all of the longing that she had for him. They had spoken frequently on the phone while she was gone, but it didn't stop them from missing each other. The night before she left, they even engaged in phone sex. Dionni was yearning for Dale to finish what they started on the phone and eagerly jumped into the shower.

Fifteen minutes later, she was en route to Dale's house. The entire drive over, Dionni trembled in anticipation. Since the two started seeing each other again, they had not engaged in any physical behavior. It was extremely hard for both of them, but Dionni didn't want to fall back into the trance of Dale's lovemaking melody.

Dionni couldn't fake the funk anymore and act like she did not want Dale as badly as he confided that he wanted her during their telephone lovemaking session. While on the phone, Dale confided to Dionni that he understood what Raheem Devaughn meant when he sang the words to his song "Empty." He was love sick and empty without Dionni. Dale also apologized again for everything. He was completely out of line for searching the world for what he always had at home. He ensured her that when she returned he was going to show her that he realized his mistakes.

Walking up to Dale's door, Dionni took a deep breath and rang the door bell. Dale answered the door and quickly swooped Dionni into his arms. He was so happy to see her. After their embrace, Dale took a step back and closed the door.

Dionni noticed that Dale was wearing a wife beater, a pair of gym shorts, and an apron.

"Please have a seat, ma'am, and enjoy your breakfast at Café Dale."

Dale whisked Dionni into the dining room, where the table was set for two. He pulled out her chair and asked her to have a seat.

"Well, well, Chef Dale," Dionni said through a smile. "What's on the menu?"

A heavenly aroma was coming from the kitchen making Dionni's mouth water.

"Well, Ms. Lady. The chef has prepared steak, eggs, grits, and biscuits. He understands that it is three o'clock in the afternoon, but he knew that our guest today had a long night, and hadn't had a chance to eat anything, let alone breakfast."

Dale disappeared into the kitchen and returned with two platters full of food. Dionni was in heaven as Dale served and pampered her. Dionni was impressed. This man really took his time as he squeezed two glasses of orange juice right in front of her.

Once breakfast was over, Dale escorted Dionni into his bedroom. "Empty" was playing in the background on repeat.

*Dale really put in a lot of effort today*, Dionni thought.

There were rose petals sprinkled on the bed, and on his dresser were two champagne glasses with a bottle of Dom P chilling in a tub of ice.

Dale closed the door behind them and kissed Dionni tenderly on her neck. Goosebumps covered her entire body. Dionni was just speechless. Not allowing her to speak, Dale retrieved a bag that was hidden on the side of his bed.

"I got something for you," he said, handing her the bag. Opening it, Dionni began to tremble again. She pulled out a dozen roses and a card. She opened the card and began to read Dale's handwritten words:

*Dionni, I have prayed for this day to come again. I thank God everyday for opening up your heart and giving me another chance. I don't want anyone else in my world, and I truly believe that God sent an angel to me and named her Dionni. Baby, will you marry me? Please think about it. Please do not give me a fast no. I rather take a slow yes.*

Tears streamed from Dionni's eyes as she looked up to see Dale handing her a small box. "Baby, please open it."

Dionni followed his directions and slowly opened the box. Inside was a five-carat pear shaped platinum diamond ring. Before she could answer, Dale tenderly placed his finger in front of her mouth and asked her not to respond.

"I want you to take your time before answering. I really want you to be sure that this is really what you want." Nodding that she understood, Dionni placed all of the items back into the bag.

Dale wrapped his arms around her and said softly, "Thank you. Thank you for giving me this opportunity to hold you again. You feel so good. Baby, you are so beautiful."

They stood in silence for several more seconds

just holding each other. Dionni looked up into his eyes and said, "Baby, I love you."

Longing to hear those words out of her mouth again, Dale leaned down and kissed Dionni passionately, rubbing and caressing her entire body.

Dale lifted Dionni and placed her onto the bed, slowly undressing her. Dionni didn't argue, and softly asked him to make love to her. Not waiting for her to change her mind, Dale gladly accepted the responsibility of that task.

The sun was beginning to set when Dale and Dionni finally let up for air. Frankly, the only reason why they were getting up anyway was that Dale had a meeting at seven. Dionni did not want to leave, but Dale always understood and supported her busy schedule, so she had to do the same.

They showered together where a quickie took place. It was six-thirty, and Dionni did not want Dale to be late.

Giving him a kiss bye, Dionni promised Dale that once his meeting was over he could come over and they could go for round two. Grabbing her bag, Dionni kissed Dale again, and quickly left.

Dionni stopped at the office to pick up her mail. Tiana wasn't there, so she took a picture of all of the items in the bag from the camera on her phone, one by one by. Dionni did not know exactly how Tiana felt about her and Dale.

Dionni left the office and started her trek home. Ding. The gas light on her dashboard came on. Stopping at a Chevron, Dionni reached in the back of her passenger seat to grab her purse off the floor. She felt nothing.

"Fuck!" Dionni said after searching the entire back seat for her purse. Trying to retrace her steps, Dionni thought carefully of where she was last with the purse. When she went into her office, she only needed her keys so she didn't leave it there.

"I must have left it at Dale's," she said to herself as she dialed his number. The phone just rang and went to voice mail.

"Hey, babe, it's me. I know you must be in your meeting, and I apologize. I am on my way back to your house to look around for my purse. I think I left it. I am going to see if Twan can let me in. When you get this message give me a call back. My gas light just came on, and I have no cash or cards. Talk to you in a minute.

Bye."

Dionni tried his number a couple more times and kept getting the voicemail.

*I hope Twan is there or I got to call Geico. Damn, I wish he still had the keypad on the garage. I could have just run in and out really quickly. It's almost eight. Hopefully we will be pulling up at the same time.*

# *Chapter 14*

"Hey, I am outside," a woman said to Dale through the phone. Dionni had just left, and Dale was worn out. He made love to her so many times in the past, but never was it as intense for him as it was today. Dale decided to catch a few shut eyes before he got up and got ready for his meeting, but lost track of the time. Not looking at the Caller ID, Dale answered the phone with his face buried in the pillow.

"Okay, give me a minute. I'll be right out."

"Damn, it's seven-fifteen already?" Dale said under his breath. He jumped up and pulled on a pair of jeans and a shirt. Slipping on his slippers, he walked out to meet his guest. It was a woman, but Dale could not catch her voice.

Nia sat in her Daewoo wondering what the hell was going on. Dale called her yesterday and asked her could she come by. Before that it had been a couple of weeks since the last time they spoke.

Nia and Dale had been messing around on and off for about a year and a half and Nia knew about Dionni. He was up front with her when she came over Antwan and Dale's house one night with Alicia. He told her that he had a girlfriend, so if they were going to kick it then it would be in her best interest not to catch feelings. He ensured her that he was not leaving his girl, so falling in love was not an option.

Nia told him that it was cool and informed him that all she was trying to do was have fun. This brotha was fine as hell, so she was just going to enjoy herself. Nia had three kids and was looking for a Captain Save a Ho. At first the situation was cool, but after kicking it with Dale a couple of times, she couldn't help but catch feelings.

He had the complete package: House, car, and job. All the fools that she had been messing with either lived with their baby mamas or at home with their own mamas. They were always asking her for money to borrow, or she had to pick them up because they never had a car.

They were always an aspiring rapper, producer, drug dealer, pimp, or all of the above. Nia promised herself that she had to step up her game and find herself a real man, so when she came across Dale, she was not going to let that go that easily. Since they started fucking, Nia had always forgotten something over there. A pair of panties here, a bra there, but never had Dionni found anything.

Nia figured Dale must have inspected the house thoroughly before Dionni came over because Dionni never knew about her. Since Dale and Dionni broke up, he started to kick it more with Nia. In her mind, she just knew that they were starting to get serious. Sooner or later, Alicia and Antwan would be getting their own place and Nia and her kids could move in. That would be the day! Then, just like that…No Dale.

Dale told Nia in the beginning that she should never pop up at his shit and like the good side chick that she was, she followed his directions. Nia used to like being Dale's side dish and felt honored when he told her that she was his appetizer. But after spending a couple of months as Dale's main squeeze, Nia has halfway going crazy.

Alicia didn't make it any better telling her that Dionni was back in the picture. Alicia was always at their house and would report back to her everything that she saw Dale do for Dionni. How he spent almost every night over her house, or how he would be on the phone talking to her saying how much he loved and missed her as he walked by Alicia and Antwan watching television.

After what felt like an eternity, Dale finally

ame outside, interrupting her thoughts. Unlocking the door, Nia signaled for Dale to get in. She was hoping that they were going to go do something, but when she looked down at his slipper clad feet, Nia knew otherwise. Dale was Mr. GQ and would never go anywhere in some house shoes. Sighing, Nia sat back into her seat and said, "Hey."

"What's good wit' it?" Dale had rehearsed this conversation so many times in his head. But with Nia sitting right next to him looking and smelling sexy as ever, he was at a loss for words.

"Nothing, baby, just missing you. What's up? Did I do something wrong?" Nia stared at the steering wheel. *If he wants to play house with that girl, then go ahead*, she thought. *I just hope he don't dismiss me completely. We can go back to how things were. I hope Alicia was just spicing things up.*

Alicia had been at the house a couple of times when Dionni came over, so Dale knew that Nia had an idea of what was going on in his life. But Dale had never not called her. Dale liked Nia, but always knew that it was never going to be a relationship. He liked that she was so submissive, but that same virtue was why Dale did not want her.

Nia was fine and made his toes curl, but at the end of the day that was it. Nia wanted nothing out of life besides to get her hair and nails done, and go shopping at Factory to You. Nia had *three* daughters already, by three different men and this was also a no no in Dale's book. He was not ready to be play step daddy, and the only woman that he wanted to be the mother of his children, he asked to marry him.

"Well, I can see the confusion behind your eyes, and I am sorry that I have been the cause of that, but I have something that I have to tell you," he began. "We have been cool for so long so I thought that it would be better if I told you this myself. I know that you know Dionni is back in my life. You have always had my back, but from the beginning, I have always been completely one hundred with you, so I am not going to start lying now. "

Dale paused to see how well Nia was taking in everything he said. He knew she was searching for a real man, but Dale knew he was not the one for her. Honestly, he looked at Nia and the rest of the other chickens that he fucked around with like a notch in his bed. The only reason he was explaining *anything* to Nia was because of Alicia. He felt uncomfortable everyday she was at his house. The first night Dionni came over and Alicia was there, Dale was nervous as hell. He knew he did not owe either one of these bitches an explanation, but didn't like the daggers Alicia kept shooting him or Dionni whenever they walked into the room. He knew if he did not nip this shit in the bud right now, it was going to smoke in the city, and he did not want to have to catch a case killing a hood rat.

"Well anyway, I am telling you all of this because I want us to still be friends. My girl and I are trying to work things out. That is why you haven't heard from me. I have fucked up in the past, and I am just trying to do things different this time. It is just important for you to understand what I am saying. I just asked D to marry me."

Tears began to flow from Nia's eyes. She clutched the steering wheel tightly, trying to compose herself. Nia turned and looked at Dale. "You asked her to marry you? Uh um, congratulations, I guess. I have been so lonely without you. Where do we go from here? I am willing to do whatever you want to do. I have been so uninspired to do anything without knowing what is going on between us. Dale, baby, I need you."

On cue, Nia reached over and planted a soft kiss

on Dale's lips. She ran her hand down his chest softly until she reached her favorite section of his body. Meticulously she caressed him until she felt the tool that she knew so well begin to grow.

Momentarily forgetting that he was supposed to be calling things off with Nia, his hand automatically ventured up to her breast. Hearing the sound of a car horn interrupted the two. Jerking back, Dale knew he had fucked up.

"What the hell am I doi--" Dale started to say before he glanced over Nia's shoulder and saw the image of Dionni's BMW staring back at him.

"Fuck," Dale yelled. "Dionni is going to kill us." This shit was not supposed to happen. He told this girl to come over so he could explain to her that this was the last time that they were going to meet up like this, but here he go fucking up again.

Nia had never seen Dionni up close. She was more curious of what she looked like than being scared that she caught them in the act.

To preoccupied trying to catch a glimpse of Dionni, Nia did not hear Dale at first tell her to drive off.

"Nia, do you fucking hear me? Pull the hell off," Dale yelled, slightly hysterical. "Pull off, please."

He was bouncing around in the seat, sitting straight up to see what Dionni was doing. Then he slumped down, hoping she did not see him in the passenger seat. Dionni had seen Nia's car before in the past. She had picked Dale up a couple of times with while Nia has been kicking back at the house. Dale would just stay on the phone with her until she arrived and would just walk out. A couple of times Dionni asked him whose car was it, and he always acted as if he did not know.

"Antwan has company," would be his answer every time. Now he was sitting here kissing a girl who was supposed to be Antwan's friend. How did this shit look? Dale was panicking now.

"Nia, please just go."

Finally Nia started up the car and backed out of the driveway. But instead of going in the opposite direction of Dionni's car, Nia did the most hateful thing that Dale could think of. She drove in the direction of Dionni's car. As they drove past, Dale caught Dionni's hurt and confused expression.

# *Chapter 15*

Not able to move, Dionni was flabbergasted by what she just witnessed. Dale was a real piece of work! He did not just propose to her earlier that day and was now kissing some bitch in front of his house!

Calming down, Dionni tried to make sure that she did not do anything irrational. *This fool got me so fucked up! And to think, I was going to tell him yes!*

"Ain't this a bitch?" Dionni exclaimed, dumbfounded by what just happened. Shaking it off, Dionni pulled out her cell and dialed Tiana's number. It felt like an eternity passed before Tiana finally answered. Dionni could barely speak by the way her heart was breaking.

"Hello," Tiana said for the third time, becoming aggravated. She knew that it was Dionni's number, but on the other end, there was only silence.

"T, it's me." Dionni was busting a u-turn in the street and was starting to follow Dale and this broke down broad. "Um, I just wanted to give you a heads up." Dionni sped up to catch them, forgetting that she was on E. "You have my bank card for miscellaneous expenses still, right?"

"Uh, yeah," Tiana said, confused, "why?"

"I just wanted to make sure because you might need to bail me out of jail."

Dale looked back and saw Dionni chasing them. His eyes grew wide as he turned to Nia and yelled, "Hurry up."

They raced down Camino El Norte doing eighty miles per hour. Dionni prayed that North Town wouldn't catch them. As much shit as she was talking, she really was not ready to be locked up tonight unless she went for fucking Dale up.

"Dionni, what the hell are you talking about?" Tiana asked as she pulled on a pair of sweats. Tiana knew that it would only be a matter of time before Dale fucked up, but she didn't expect it to happen so quickly. "D, don't be doing no crazy ass shit. Where the hell are you?" Tiana rushed out of her house and jumped into her Chrysler 300.

"I am following Dale and some bitch in that gold Daewoo that I told you about. He so full of shit telling me that was one of Antwan's hoes. This some shit right here. He asked me to marry him this morning, girl, and everything. I forgot my purse over there and pulled up to see these mothafuckas out here kissing and shit right in front of his house. I just made a right onto Gowan by Eva's old house. Now she turned on Scott Robinson. Where the hell she going? Wal-Mart?"

Dionni looked at her gauges on the dashboard. It read zero miles till empty. "Fuck. Tiana, I don't have any money. Can you please meet me at the gas station on Craig and Simmons? I don't have my purse or any gas. Please, T."

Dionni pulled into the gas station and sat in her car in defeat. "Why does this shit keep happening to me, T? Why? Dale can't keep his dick to himself, and Zay is a pimp. What a great combination. Is something wrong with me, T? What the hell is wrong with me?"

Tiana could only decipher pieces of what a sobbing Dionni was saying. It didn't matter at all that Dionni distanced her out of the relationship between her and Dale. None of that shit mattered right now. D needed her, and she was going to have her back through this shit. That is what she signed up for.

Tiana agreed and told her that she was on her way. She stayed on the phone with her friend, listening to her pour her heart out in agony. She decided this was the best time to tell Dionni the truth about Dale.

Sighing a sigh in relief, Dale's heart slowed down a notch when he watched Dionni pull into the gas station. He had never seen Dionni like this and was scared of what the aftermath was going to be if she did catch up with them.

Dale looked at Nia in disgust. Even when he was trying to do right, Dale let another bitch get entangled in his relationship with Dionni. "Why the hell did you kiss me?" he screamed. "I told you that I was getting married, and that is how you congratulate me? How the hell am I supposed to explain this? Bitch, is you crazy? Take me home right now!"

"How the hell are you yelling at me and you kissed me back, feeling on my titties and shit? Are you sure getting married to her is the right thing to do? You see how crazy she just acted? She almost hit us a couple of times. I don't think she is the one for you."

*That bitch is crazy,* Nia thought to herself, replaying everything that just happened in her head. *I guess I'd be mad, too, if I saw my man tongue-lashing another female right after he proposed to me. From what I could see, she ain't all that anyway. The only thing that she got over me is difference in cars that we drive.*

Nia was skeptical about taking Dale back to his

house. She was not sure if the crazy bitch would be sitting out front waiting for him. "How 'bout you call Twan, and I take you to him. I don't want to go back to your house and your bitch out there waiting for you."

Nia wasn't ready for what happened next. Dale grabbed her by the neck and pushed her head back into the seat. "Don't you ever refer to Dionni as a bitch to me again. Matter of fact, don't call me anymore. Please. Dionni was right. If I am going to cheat on her, I need to at least make sure that the broad is at least at a higher caliber than she is. And you know what, Nia, that sure ain't you. Let me out right here. I'm straight."

Dale called Twan and told him the situation. "I'm on Decatur and Craig, in the Goodwill shopping center. Call me when you are close."

Dale got out of the car, not saying two words to Nia. He was lost in thought trying to figure out how he was going to make this shit better. Right now, he was not seeing any light at the end of this tunnel. What the hell was he going to do? Disgusted, he slammed Nia's car door and walked away.

Tiana followed Dionni to her house. She was trying to figure out the best way to tell her friend what she witnessed some years back. Tiana pulled into Dionni's driveway after Dionni entered the garage. She got out of the car and followed her into the house. Dionni disappeared upstairs and Tiana remained downstairs in the living room.

A few moments later, Dionni reappeared, carrying Dior and wearing a nightgown. She was completely exhausted. It was written all over her face. Tiana met her at the fireplace, welcoming her into open arms, and Dionni fell right into them. They shared a silent conversation in that hug, allowing the flowing tears to speak to each other, comforting and consoling one another.

Tiana broke the silence. "Girl, got me up in here crying and shit. You scared me today. I thought I really was going to have to get you out of lock up. If that would have happened, I would have paid your bail, and then went over there to go Madea on his trifling black ass."

They sat down on the couch, wiping tears away while laughing. Even though she was laughing, mentally, Dionni really did not know what was going to happen from here.

"D, what happened with you and Zay? He just

disappeared out of your life. You mentioned that he was a pimp on the phone. Are you serious, girl? What happened?"

Tiana was going to tell Dionni the truth about Dale, but couldn't help but ask, especially after Dionni's breakdown on the phone.

Tiana was going to wait for Dionni to bring it up, but how many months had it been since Dale was back into the picture? Tiana couldn't wait that long.

Feeling guilty, Tiana paused. Maybe she shouldn't pry. If Dionni wanted to talk about it, then she would bring it up.

Surprisingly, Dionni didn't hesitate and told Tiana everything. She told her the entire story of what happened in Detroit, him leaving the note at her house for them to talk, and how all of this led up to the discovery that she made in Zay's living room.

Tiana shook her head. "Gurl." No wonder her friend jumped back into a relationship with Dale feet first. That was some crazy shit. "So has he tried to see you since then? I know he has called you, but have you seen him?"

"You know what, not lately," Dionni said thinking back to when was the last time she heard from

Zay. She had been so wrapped up in Dale, that she lost a sense for time for anything outside of her business and Dale.

"I guess he is finally getting the picture. The thing is both of these fools don't realize I want to have to compete with another female in my relationship. I don't want to understand what she is going through and why she needs you to come when she calls or just listen. I feel that if I am giving a hundred percent to you, then why is it a crime for me to expect the same thing back?"

Tiana listened to her girl, and gave a soft "Amen" when she was finished. *I think now is the best time for me to tell her.* Tiana took in a deep breath.

"D, I have something to tell you," she started off, looking Dionni in the eyes. "Well, you know that I had to let Antwan go a while back. I really didn't talk about it much because you were still adjusting getting back on track after the baby."

Dionni nodded at her friend with a sad face, reliving the pain endured from losing her baby.

Tiana continued. "Well, I want to start off by saying that I really did want for Antwan and I to work. We broke up for other reasons bigger than our relationship. A lot of shit happened that night you lost the baby. Because you were in your situation, I felt that getting you back on track was the most important thing. Everything else could be handled later."

Dionni did not like the way that Tiana kept going around the subject. "Okay, T. I understand that everyone was worried about me. I am sorry if I put a stress on your friendship. I am so s-" Tiana put her hands up, summoning Dionni to be quiet.

"Girl, this shit had nothing to do with you, per se. The final factor that broke me and Antwan up was Antwan. We didn't last because I wasn't happy with the way Antwan handled a particular situation with Dale. I felt that if he didn't step up and check his brother, then he must be doing the same thing."

Tiana was still beating around the bush. Dionni pleaded with Tiana's eyes coaxing Tiana to just tell her what happened.

Inhaling again, Tiana started her story again. "The night that you lost the baby, I picked Antwan up from work because he locked the keys into the car. I drove him to Dale's so that he could get his spare key because you two were supposed to go to Cancun, remember?"

Dionni nodded. "Well, Twan had to pee, so I

punched the code to get in by the garage door. I went downstairs to get the keys off the rack and walked into - --" Tiana stopped not wanting to describe the scene that she saw take place that night.

"What, T? You walked into what?" Dionni already knew what direction the story was going in. She just wanted Tiana to tell her what happened.

"Well, girl," Tiana began again tearing up while she spoke, "I saw Dale fucking two females in the game room. The coldest part about it is he knew I saw him. The bitches had him too occupied, but Antwan told him I was there.

"Antwan and I left the house and started to argue about who should tell you, and then you called and said that you needed me. After that, your well being was my main concern. That's why I was short with Dale in the hospital. You probably didn't notice but I was. I wanted you to get well and past your loss. I felt like it was a blessing in disguise. Since then, I really didn't care too much for Dale."

Happy that she finally got it all out, Tiana cried to herself for a moment. She cried because she was disappointed in herself that it took her this long to tell Dionni what happened. She cried because of the relief that she felt in her heart. But lastly, Tiana cried for the pain she knew she just administered on her friend.

Dionni didn't move or say anything. She just stared at the rug, lost in thought. Dionni was speechless. So many questions were running through her head. She wanted to be mad at Tiana, but how could she? Tiana was trying to be a friend. If the shoe was on the other foot, what would Dionni do? It was crazy, but probably the same exact thing.

"Why didn't you tell me all of this before? So he didn't see you? Did you see the girls' faces? Do we know who they are? Girl, my head is hurting. I think I need to lie down."

Dionni's stomach began to turn. "I can't win for losing. Zay is a pimp and Dale, I don't know what to say about him. This is crazy. I need to leave the whole bunch of them alone. I had to start from scratch so many times before, and right now I do have a problem doing that all over again."

Dale was going out of his mind because he did not know what to do. He didn't know where the hell Dionni's head was at. While waiting for Antwan, Dale decided it might be best if he waited till the next day before he attempted to call her. By the time Antwan pulled up, Dale felt really somber. He knew he was completely foul in this situation. He was known for being a dog in the past but damn, this time was different. This time though, he was trying to do right.

Dale gave Twan the short version of everything that went down. Twan didn't say anything. Shit, he really didn't know what to say about it. They drove the rest of the way in silence.

Once at home, Dale lay across the bed and finally listened to his messages. His mailbox was full. There were a couple of messages from Dionni telling him that she forgot her purse and was on her way back. If only he answered the phone, he wouldn't be in this predicament. He was too caught up in breaking it off with Nia completely that he put his cell phone on silent.

Then there were a few messages from Nia. "Baby, I am so sorry. I should have listened to you. I was scared, Dale. I thought you were leaving me. Baby, we can talk about it."

Dale became disgusted listening to her cry.

*What the fuck is she crying for? Fuck that bitch!*

Dale deleted every one of her messages from his inbox without even listening to them. The final message came from a private number. He had to replay the message a couple of times before he caught the voice.

"Dale, it's me. When you get this message please call me back. We need to talk."

Dale went cold turkey from Ashley when he left Nia and the others alone.

*What does she want? I haven't heard from her in a minute.*

Dale decided against calling Ashley or Nia back. He just needed some time to think. Reaching over to turn on the television, Dale spotted Dionni's purse hanging on the door. Why didn't he notice it earlier? A constant beat played a rhythm in Dale's temples. Deciding to deal with this shit in the morning, Dale closed his eyes and went to sleep.

"Hi, I would like some pamphlets and brochures on the events that you coordinate, and price quotes." Candy entered Whateva You Like Entertainment after carefully scoping the perimeter first. Making sure that Dionni's car was no where in sight, Candy finally decided to enter the premises.

"The pamphlets and brochures are over there, but if you want detailed information, you have to make an appointment with the owner, Dionni Stone." Tiana was trying to help the customer, but was interrupted when Dale walked in. "Ma'am, please check out the information, and if there is anything else that I can do to be of assistance, please let me know. My name is Tiana."

Turning her attention to Dale, Tiana asked, "How may I help you?"

*What balls he got coming in here.* Tiana thought. She folded her arms across her chest and looked him up and down.

"T, is Dionni here? I need to talk to her." Dale shifted his weight from his left leg to his right. Dale had stayed his distance from Tiana ever since that night. He was thankful she never told his secret, but he could never figure out why she would keep the secret. "She is not here, Dale." Tiana said, angry. "As I said, is there anything *I* can do for you?"

Candy sensed the animosity as she pretended to browse through the documents. Her goal was to befriend Tiana, but maybe this guy would be better bait for Dionni. Candy cleared her throat.

"Well thank you, Miss," she said. "May I have a card? Once I have decided exactly what I want, I will make an appointment with Ms. Stone."

Candy smiled as she accepted the card from

Tiana. She turned and started out the door, but not before she smiled seductively at Dale. Dale smiled back and turned his attention back to Tiana.

Waiting in her rental, Candy began to change her plan strategy. Her plan at first was to become friends with Tiana and get as much information about Dionni as she could. She knew Dionni's best friend worked for her from listening to Zay. She didn't know exactly what she was going to do with the information as of yet, but now it didn't matter.

Dale was Candy's new target, and she knew exactly what she could do to him. From the part of the conversation that she just witnessed, Dionni was pissed at Dale. Candy was going to have fun with fine ass at first, then make him fall in love.

Watching the front door, Candy waited only a couple more moments before Dale stormed out to his car.

On cue, Candy stepped out her vehicle and approached Dale. "Hey," she said.

Dale was pissed off by the heated conversation that he just had with Tiana. Lost in his own thoughts, Dale did not hear Candy speak to him.

"Excuse me," Candy said a little louder. Dale walked right past her and was almost at his car. He heard her voice and turned around.

"Yes," Dale said, eyeing the beautiful woman standing in front of him. She was the same lady who just smiled at him. Dale ran his fingers through his hair and waited for her to respond.

Handing him her card, Candy waited a moment before she spoke. "My name is Candy, and I noticed that you were getting agitated inside. Maybe I can help you release your tension."

Once he removed the card from her fingertips, Candy reached in and pulled Dale toward her. Kissing him gently on ear, she whispered, "I promise it will be worth the call," and walked off. Candy felt his eyes on her as she sauntered into the direction of the rental. Once inside, she turned and looked in his direction.

Seeing that he was still staring at her, Candy waved, smiled, and drove off.

# *Chapter 16*

Ding. Dionni thought she heard the doorbell, but she knew she was not expecting anyone. She just got out of the shower and was running late. David fitted her in at the last minute to style her hair. She had a dinner meeting with a potential client and was going to shoot straight there after her hair appointment.

After formulating in her head an outfit to wear, Dionni rushed into the bathroom to start getting ready.

Ding. There it went again. Checking her phone, Dionni didn't have any missed calls. Dionni continued dressing. She was rocking a black Gucci jumpsuit with gold trim. To finish it off, she stepped into a pair of black Gucci heels with gigantic gold G's on the heels. She brushed her hair back out of her face, and pulled it into a ponytail.

After grabbing Dior, her keys, and purse, then putting Dior in the kennel, Dionni proceeded down the stairs and got into her car. Waiting for the garage to open, Dionni glanced at a car through her side view mirror sitting directly across the street.

*Damn, that car looks familiar*, Dionni thought as she tried to remember where she'd seen that Chevy

Malibu at before. Shaking it off, Dionni backed out the driveway, closed the garage, and drove like a mad woman to get across town to David's shop.

Sitting under the dryer, Dionni flipped through an *Essence* magazine. Absorbed in the magazine, Dionni didn't notice the figure nervously watching her from the front of the salon.

David noticed the stranger as soon as she came in. He thought she was a walk-in because he'd never seen her before. She was nappy by the head, and David was *certain* that she came in for some servicing. The wig was knotted and tangled, and she had the nerve to have a dirty bandana tied around it. David started to inform her that she had to make an appointment because he had taken his last client for the day, but concluded very quickly that his expertise was not her main objective.

Indecisively, Ashley was apprehensive of what exactly should she do. Should she just walk over and talk to Dionni or should she just walk out the door. She inhaled, pushed her shoulders back, and walked over to Dionni.

The closer Ashley got to the dryers, the harder her heart began to beat in her chest. Part of her wanted to leave well enough alone, but something in her gut told her otherwise. Ashley hoped her plan worked.

Dionni glanced up from her magazine and noticed Ashley coming her way.

*Damn, she looks familiar. Where do I know her from?*

Dionni was terrible with names, but she always remembered a face. She knew that if she thought hard enough it was going to come back to her. Ashley caught Dionni's eyes and slowly began to smirk as she gained more confidence. She figured Dionni was spooked seeing her. Little did she know, Dionni was feeling the complete opposite.

Stopping directly in front of Dionni, Ashley crossed her arms across her chest and looked Dionni up and down. Her actions startled Dionni because she still couldn't place where she knew this chick from. Sensing all the animosity rise from this girl made Dionni uncomfortable. Getting up from under the dryer, Dionni sat the magazine down on the rack.

"Hey, Dionni, how are you?"

"I'm good, ma. Do I know you from somewhere?" Dionni glared back at her.

"Well, I guess it has been awhile since you saw

me. My name is Ashley. Does that sound familiar?"

Ashley took a step back and smacked her lips. She didn't know what to expect from Dionni. If this girl was gonna try to fight her, she had to be ready.

"Yeah, you look familiar, but I really don't remember from where. From the way you are mad dogging me though, I feel that you are going to remind me."

Watching the girl approach Dionni, David thought that it would be in everyone's best intentions if he intervened. He did not know exactly what was brewing, but he could tell that it was going to leave a bad taste in someone's mouth. If this girl knew anything about Dionni, she knew that it was going to be hers.

"Excuse me, Miss Lady. The salon is closed. I am not taking anymore customers." David stepped in between the women and faced Ashley.

"No, sir. You can not help me with anything, but I think Dionni can." Ashley said this slowly and with much attitude.

Slightly, David turned and glanced at Dionni. He gave Dionni a *do you know her* look.

Dionni responded to Ashley, not paying David any mind.

"What do you mean I can help you? I can help you with what?"

Dionni was starting to get pissed off. She hated when people played games with their words. "Again, what can I help you with?"

"I guess you don't remember me. My name is Ashley. About a year ago, we had a confrontation at Dale's house. Do you remember me now?"

Ashley cut her eyes from David to Dionni, smirking.

Dionni started to chuckle. "That's where I know you from! David, this is the chicken that was hiding in the garage."

David and Dionni looked at each other, and both busted out laughing.

"Are you serious right now?" Dionni asked almost in tears. "What the hell do you want from me, Ms. Ashley?"

Ashley didn't know what to say. She wanted Dionni to be upset that she confronted her, but laughing? Ashley was not prepared for this one.

"Well, ugh—I wanted to inform you of some important information you can pass on to Dale. I am pregnant. He is about to be a daddy."

There. She said it.

Ashley began to fidget. Ashley had an entire speech memorized that she wanted to say to Dionni, but now she was at a loss of words.

Dionni stared Ashley down, becoming upset. "Ma, let me ask you a question? And for real. Woman to woman. What the hell does that have to do with me? How did you find me? And why do think you being pregnant is any of my concern?"

Dionni's voice elevated with every word. She kept her composure in her stance, but was boiling on the inside. The other two women in the salon began looking in their direction. David intervened and told Dionni and Ashley to go into his office.

"Excuse me, y'all. I will be right back." He informed his customers and locked the front door.

David turned on the office light and told them to both to have a seat. "I believe you both have a lot to talk about," David started off. "Ashley, that is your name, right? I don't know what you were trying to accomplish telling my girl that you are pregnant, and truthfully that is not my business. I am going to close the door, and let you two talk in private. Holla if you need me, D."

Dionni nodded at David and he left the room.

Sitting down behind David's desk, Dionni took a deep breath. "Let me start off by again by asking you this. How did you know to find me here? And again, why are you telling me, and not Dale?"

Dionni sat in the chair and waited on her response.

*Pregnant? I feel like I am going to be sick,* Dionni thought.

Dionni kept her game face on as she glared at Ashley. Dionni felt weak and clenched the arms of the chair.

Dionni knew the rule of never showing your opponent that you are defeated, so she expressed no emotion to Ashley. She was not going to let this girl know that she just got the best of her. She always believed she would be the mother of Dale's kids.

Ashley felt Dionni's negative energy generating from across the desk. She did not know where to begin. She wanted Dionni to feel just as hurt as she did, but telling from her demeanor, the only thing Ashley did was piss Dionni off.

"Ashley, are you going to answer my question, or what?" Dionni was getting annoyed by Ashley's sudden need to become silent. "I have a meeting with a client, and I need to finish getting my hair together. I do not have all day."

Dionni beamed so much hate through her eyes at Ashley. *If this girl does not hurry up and speak, pregnant or not, I am going to whoop her ass.*

Clearing her throat, Ashley said, "Well to answer your first question, I knew you were here because I followed you here."

"You followed me?" Dionni asked, disgusted. *This bitch has really lost her mind. I'm gonna have to have her pregnant ass arrested for harassment.* "Go on and finish your story. I think this is going to be good."

"I sat in front of your house for about thirty minutes before I finally got the courage to ring the doorbell. I started to leave, but I swore I heard something or someone move around in the house."

"Oh, so you are the one that was ringing the doorbell?" Dionni said under her breath. She began to rock in the chair, nodding as she listened.

"Yes, when I received no response I figured you must have seen me through the peep hole and was trying to ignore me. That is why I felt I followed you here because I really needed to tell you this."

"What makes you think I give a hell that you are

pregnant? What does that have to do with me? That is between you and that nigga. I am so burnt out on him because I am tired of dealing with petty ass bitches like you."

"How did you know where I lived? Did that negro tell you where I lived?"

Dionni's rocking intensified as she waited for Ashley to respond. She stared into space with a blank look on her face

"No. Dale doesn't know anything about this. I followed him from his house to yours one night. I haven't spoken to him in two and a half months. Not since you worked your way back into his life. We were beginning to be happy, and here you come. Dale and I actually established a relationship. Then just like that," Ashley snapped her fingers, "he was gone. Why you couldn't leave well enough alone?"

Ashley was yelling now at the top of her lungs. She appeared as if she was going to lunge at Dionni across the table. David came back in the room.

By this time, Dionni had stood and removed the towel from around her shoulders. David saw she was ready to pounce at any moment and grabbed her before she did something she would regret.

"Leave well enough alone," Dionni yelled at Ashley, trying to get around David. "Dale came back to me just like he always does. If I was able to get back in the picture like that, then he wasn't yours in the first place. I know this. You better take your pregnant ass up out of here before I choke the shit out of you."

"Yes, Ms. Lady," David added, still holding onto Dionni, "you need to leave before I call the police and have you arrested for trespassing."

"And speaking of the police, I am going to file charges against you for stalking. If I ever see you or that busted ass Malibu around my house, or even in my neighborhood, I will have you in jail for stalking. Do you hear me? I hate low self esteem ass broads like you."

With tears running down her face, Ashley walked out of the salon defeated. David followed Ashley to the front door, dragging Dionni by the arm, and locked it. He watched Ashley get in her car and finally pull off.

Once he was for certain she was gone, David finally let Dionni go. She had tears running down her face. David didn't know what to say. Dale was out of Dionni's life and was still hurting his friend. How come he had so much power over her?

Dionni hurried and gathered her purse and keys. Pulling her hair back into a ponytail, Dionni informed David that she was going to pay him later.

"Ms. Thing, where are you going? You better not be trying to find that girl. She ain't worth it. Yo-"

Dionni unlocked the door and interrupted him with a kiss on his cheek.

"Baby, don't worry. I am not going to mess with that girl. I am going to look for Dale." She walked out of the shop.

Dionni pulled up to Dale's house and sat for a moment. She haven't spoken or seen him since the high speed chase. Dionni cried the entire ride over there. She was so hurt that Ashley was pregnant.

Dionni knew there was always a possibility that Dale had kids out in the world, but damn. To actually have the pregnancy confirmed...Dionni felt numb. When she was pregnant and losing her baby, Dale was having a ménage trois. Just the thought made Dionni queasy all over again.

Dale's car was outside. Dionni tried to call him but his phone went straight to voicemail. She got out of her car and walked to the door.

A feeling of déjà vu came over Dionni. The hair on her arms and the back of her neck rose. Shaking it off, Dionni rang the doorbell. She waited a few moments and didn't receive a response.

Reaching in to knock on the door, Dionni realized the door was not all the way closed. She tried the knob, but it was locked.

She contemplated just going in, but she rang the doorbell again instead. After a few more moments and no response, Dionni pushed the door open and walked inside.

"Dale." Dionni called his name as she walked down the stairs to the game room. Something was not right. A cold chill ran through her body. When she reached the bottom of the stairs, she called his name again. Finding no one there, Dionni breathed a sigh of relief.

Coming back up the stairs, Dionni heard a noise. It sounded like a slight moan. Dionni stopped in her tracks. She called Dale's name again.

There was still no response. Something told her to leave, but Dionni went against her better judgment and walked down the hallway to his room.

The closer she got to the door, the louder the moans became. She was certain Dale was in there but wasn't sure if he was alone or not.

Slowly she turned the door knob, trembling with every motion.

*Maybe he's watching a porno*, Dionni tried to convince herself.

"Ah, D-a-l-e." These words came in between sounds of moaning and gurgling.

Dionni pushed the door open and was shocked by the scene that was taking place in Dale's bed. It was dark in the room, so Dionni had to wait for her eyes to adjust. Dale and the woman were so wrapped up in each other they did not notice Dionni standing in the doorway at first.

The pair was in the sixty-nine position. The woman was lying on her back and Dale was straddled above her going to town in between her straddled legs. He was so lost in sucking, licking, and fingering his company that he did not pay attention to Dionni coming closer.

Dale's body began gyrating and he collapsed on top of the woman's body as he came in the woman's mouth and face.

"Baby, I thought you said you were going to let me know before you were gonna cum," the woman said, laughing. She sat up and tried to push him off of her.

All sounds of laughter suddenly went away as the woman opened her eyes and saw Dionni standing damn near over the bed.

"Dale, get up."

"Baby, what's wrong? I know you are not--" Dale couldn't finish his sentence. He finally spotted Dionni standing there.

"D!"

"I'm sorry I interrupted." Dionni started with a new set of tears flowing down her face. "I just came to tell you that Ashley followed me to David's to tell me she's having your baby. You better call her. Congratulations…Daddy. The door was open, that's why I came in."

Dionni paused and took in a deep breath. Neither one of them attempted to move a muscle. Before she caught a case, she turned and began to walk out the door.

"Tell your baby mama to stay the hell away from me," Dionni spat at Dale. She looked at the woman and said, "And, Eva, bitch, this shit ain't over."

# The

# Appetizer

Novel from the Pen of

Ni'cola

NCM Publishing

# Chapter 1

"Mommy, we hungry, and there ain't no milk. Mommy, wake up!"

I opened my eye a crack and moaned. I had a long night, and this girl was really blowing my high. My eight-year-old daughter stood over me with her baby sister Jade on her hip.

"Be quiet, girl, shit!" I snapped at my eldest. Sometimes I think this girl forgets that I am the momma and she is the kid. I had to admit that Sky was a really big help with her sisters, but right now I was not in the mood to be sentimental.

I rolled over onto my stomach and rubbed the sleep out of my eyes. I just barely fell asleep about an hour ago and here this lil' nigga comes demanding me to get up! What I wouldn't give for a chance to sleep in on a Saturday morning like the mothafuckas on TV.

"Mommy, I am sorry for waking you up," Sky said not sounding too empathetic. "Jade don't have no more diapers, and there ain't no milk in the fridge. I was gonna give her a cup and make me and Lilly some cereal, but I couldn't. Can you please go to the store?

All of us are hungry."

Sky transferred my chunky twenty-month-old baby from her left hip to the right, staring me down. Rolling her eyes at me, Sky bounced and soothed Jade, who began to whine because she wanted me to get her. I was about to slap the shit out of Sky, but then realized why my daughter was jumping bad with me.

The cover slipped off me, and I only had on my bra with no panties. Pulling the blanket back over me, I ordered for them to get out. "Give me a minute to get dressed, and I'll run to the store real quick. Okay?" Sky nodded her head and stormed out in disgust, slamming the door behind her. I shook my head and rolled back over in the bed.

Gary didn't need me to get completely naked this morning when he called me saying that he was outside. He just got back into town and was on his way home to his anxiously waiting wife and son. He was craving for some of my butterscotch and informed me of this when I opened the door letting him in.

I barely pulled my night shirt over my head before he was already opening a pack of Lifestyle condoms with his teeth. Pulling his dick out of his pants, he commanded for me to suck it. Dropping to my knees,

I tenderly took his dick and placed it into my mouth. Pulling my titties out of the bra, he fondled my swelling breast as he violently pumped his dick into my mouth damn near causing me to choke.

I was missing Gary so much and asked him to stop by on his way home, but did not know that he was about to treat me like a five-dollar hoe that worked the streets. Turning me over onto all fours, Gary slapped that condom on his Johnson and let loose into me.

At first he pushed my thong to the side, but after complaining that the material was rubbing against his dick, Gary told me to take it off. After a couple more pumps, I felt Gary tense up and begin digging his nails into my hips meaning that the brother was about to climax.

Once he reached his ecstasy, Gary wobbled into the bathroom with his pants pushed midway down his thighs. Disgusted I got into the bed and began to pout. I didn't even cum, shit! I was hoping that after I broke it down to him how much I missed him, he was about to dedicate some real time to me. Look at how I was wrong.

Gary came out of the bathroom and finally decided to ask me how I was doing.

"Baby, come lay with me for a minute," I asked him, but I already knew the answer.

"Girl, you know I have to hurry and go home. I just stopped by here real quick because I know Kim got a gang of shit that she wants me to do with her tomorrow, and I ain't want to hear your mouth."

Seeing the disappointment in my face, Gary promised me that he was going to sneak back over here if Kim decided to go shopping with her friends or something. He peeled off two hundred dollar bills from the stack that he had in his pocket and gave it to me. Kissing me roughly on the cheek, Gary hurried up out the door.

Glancing at the clock it was three-thirty six. Wow a new world record. Gary's visit only lasted a total of twelve minutes. I was mad as hell, but really didn't know why. This shit was typical for me and men.

I got out the bed and made sure the door was locked. We just moved to Los Angeles from Vegas three months ago, and I was still nervous about the neighborhood. We were living in a daily weekly, which was a step higher from a motel. I was waiting for my section 8 to transfer over and couldn't afford even a cheap apartment here.

I needed a break from the bullshit that transpired back in Vegas between me and this brotha named Dale. We were messing around for over a year, but he had a girl. I started some real shit in hopes that it was going to make him leave her, but it backfired in my face. His girl left him and Dale 86ed me out of his life as well.

My home girl Yazmin was living out here with her fine as wine man Trey. She told me that I needed a change of atmosphere and offered for me to move in with the two of them till we got on our feet. I figured if she could find her a man out here, then hell so could I. Once I got my money together, I was on the first thing smoking to California.

Let me give you a brief run down of my track record with men. There were two types of niggas that pushed up on me. The first ones were the I ain't got no job, I live with my mama, I just got out of jail, I got warrants, I want to be a pimp, I am a pimp, I sell drugs, I use drugs, Baby let me hold some money till I hustle up some more, I need you to come get me 'cause I ain't got not ride type of man. The second type was the I got money, I am doing my thing, I might have kids, but I definitely got a girl or wife type man. It never failed – just those two types. No on in between came after me.

Looking at myself in the mirror, I pushed my hair back out of my face.

My name is Nia Sequoia Harris, and I am twenty-five. My momma said that my daddy was Cherokee Indian, but I ain't never met him. Oops, I am lying. She says that he used to come around a lot when I was little. But hell! I don't remember.

Some people would consider me beautiful with my creamy brown complexion and thick jet black hair that almost touched my butt. I had a banging body (even after three kids) with a flat stomach and not even one stretch mark. I was thick in all of the right places and stood almost five feet tall. I was a head turner, that's for sure, but couldn't seem to make a man stick around.

Maybe it was because I had three kids. My daughters were eight, five, and almost two. They were going to be some show stoppers when they grew up, all inheriting my smooth skin and grade of hair, but that's all that I wanted them to get from me. I wanted them to have a better relationship with the opposite sex than I did. I wanted them to empower a man, not the other way around.

*Oh well.* I shrugged my shoulders. *Can't cry over spilled milk. At least I got some money behind it.*

*And boy did I need it.* Brushing my hair into a lazy ponytail, I decided to get dressed and go do what Princess Sky commanded. I pulled on a pair of baby blue sweat pants and a matching tank top and slid on my flip flops.

"Ladies," I called for them to come out of the other bedroom and listen to my commands. "I am 'bout to run to the store and get some milk and diapers. Is there anything else that is needed 'cause when I come back, I don't want to be bothered." I added that at the end, so they could have a heads up on what type of day today was going to be.

"No, Mommy," Lilly said in her sweet and innocent voice. "We got cereal and no-noes, and Kool-Aid, so we okay." It always cracked me up how Lilly said noodles. Her lisp made her sound like a cartoon character. "Okay, baby. I'll get y'all some chips, too, okay?"

I knew this would bring a smile to all of their faces, even Sky's. "Lock the door, and don't let anyone in unless it is Auntie Yaz, okay? And if it is her, you know she will call first okay, ladies? I love you. Sky, come and lock the door."

I walked outside and could hear the locks on the

door lock behind me. I started the long trek down the stairs to the parking lot. We were on the third floor, so I was ecstatic that the girls did not have a long list. I hated lugging all of those bags up to the top floor.

Walking to my car, all eyes were on me as I swayed the fullness of my hips with every step. Men watched me wishing that I was their girl, and women turned their noses up at me hating that their man was wishing they were me. I kept my head up and smirked occasionally at the broads who were bold enough to demand eye contact from me.

Haters. I am sorry the Pussy Cat Dolls were talking about me in their song, "Don't Cha." Shaking it off, I continued on my trek. Once inside my car, I did my daily routine and said a short prayer for this car to start.

Opening my eyes, I turned the key in the ignition. I heard it hesitate, but it started. Thank you, Jesus! I put it in reverse and began my journey to the store.

I was at the light on 13th and Figueroa when this white Range Rover pulled up beside me. A light skinned brother with dreadlocks was leaning out of the window. Nodding his head to the music, he glanced over in my direction and smiled at me.

Smiling back, I proceeded to the store. Damn, I hope we were going in the same place. Turning into the parking lot of the mini mart, I took a deep breath when I seen him turn in after me. I got out of the car and thought I was trying out for Next Top Model as I walked as if on the cat walk to the front door.

Brother man with the dreds didn't park in front of the store, but pulled in front of the nail salon located in the same parking lot. Out came a big booty chick walking funny, wearing the paper flip flops they put on you when you get a pedicure. She held her hand out and on cue he loaded her palm with a stack of cash.

"Never fails," I said to myself and searched the store for what I came for. After a couple of moments, I was finished shopping and waiting at the register. Dude walked into the store and came directly up to me.

What did he want from me? I just saw his girl. What he want from me?

"Hey, ma, what's up?" Sexy dreds asked me looking finer up close. He rocked a black tank and a pair of Akidemiks Jeans. He had on black socks and black Jordan slippers. He smiled at me and pulled out a card.

"My name is Devaugn and I *had* to talk to you."

He looked me up and down and licked his lips. "What's your name, and when can I get a chance to see you again?"

The clerk interrupted our conversation, calling me to the counter. He rang everything up and recited me my total. I paid him and took my bags. Devaugn was still standing there staring at me.

"So are you going to take my card or what? I own an audio store D and S Audios just down the street from here. Call the shop or hit me up on the cell. Maybe we can discuss what can be done to upgrade that vehicle of yours."

Placing the card in between my fingertips, I had no choice but to take it.

"D and S, so the D stands for DaShawn, but what does the S stand for? I knew his name was Devaugn, but I did not want him to think I was feeling him yet. He was sexy as hell, and maybe just what I needed to get my mind off of Gary. After that session this morning, I didn't know if I could stand to look at him anymore.

"Naw, ma, my name is Devaugn not Dashawn, and the S stands for Stephanie, my wife," Devaugn said like it was written all over my face the type of men that I was destined to be with.

"Well, Mr. Devaugn, it was nice to meet you, but I do not deal with married men." I hoped God would not strike me down by telling that bold face lie to this man. I was trying to break this vicious cycle because it was not getting me anywhere.

Sashaying out of the store, I got back into my ride, and took a deep breath. "Damn he was fine! Fuck!"

Devaugn stood in the doorway of the store with a slight smile on his chiseled face.

*Damn I want him. Why men like that are only a fairytale to me? Why can't I be the one to end up with a prince charming?*

Pulling out I drove back home to my reality. Three kids, three different daddies, and no assistance.

MAR 2011

LaVergne, TN USA
11 February 2011
216221LV00003B/7/P